Ed McBain (1926–) is the pseudonym of Evan
Hunter, author of *The Blackboard Jungle* and the
screenplay for Alfred Hitchcock's *The Birds*. McBain
is a Grand Master of the Mystery Writers of America,
and is the only American writer to be awarded the
CWA Diamond Dagger for lifetime achievement.

Also by Ed McBain

The 87th Precinct Novels

COP HATER • THE MUGGER • THE PUSHER (1956) • THE CON MAN •
KILLER'S CHOICE (1957) • KILLER'S WEDGE • LADY KILLER (1958) • 'TIL
DEATH • KING'S RANSOM (1959) • GIVE THE BOYS A GREAT BIG HAND •
THE HECKLER • SEE THEM DIE (1960) • LADY, LADY, I DID IT! (1961) •
THE EMPTY HOURS • LIKE LOVE (1962) • TEN PLUS ONE (1963) • AX
(1964) • HE WHO HESITATES • DOLL (1965) • EIGHTY MILLION EYES
(1966) • FUZZ (1968) • SHOTGUN (1969) • JIGSAW (1970) • HAIL, HAIL
THE GANG'S ALL HERE! (1971) • SADIE WHEN SHE DIED • LET'S HEAR IT
FOR THE DEAF MAN (1972) • HAIL TO THE CHIEF (1973) • BREAD (1974) •
BLOOD RELATIVES (1975) • SO LONG AS YOU BOTH SHALL LIVE (1976) •
LONG TIME NO SEE (1977) • CALYPSO (1979) • GHOSTS (1980) • HEAT
(1981) • ICE (1983) • LIGHTNING (1984) • EIGHT BLACK HORSES (1985) •
POISON • TRICKS (1987) • LULLABY (1989) • VESPERS (1990) • WIDOWS
(1991) • KISS (1992) • MISCHIEF (1993) • AND ALL THROUGH THE HOUSE
(1994) • ROMANCE (1995)

The Matthew Hope Novels

GOLDILOCKS (1978) • RUMPELSTILTSKIN (1981) • BEAUTY AND THE BEAST
(1982) • JACK AND THE BEANSTALK (1984) • SNOW WHITE AND ROSE RED
(1985) • CINDERELLA (1986) • PUSS IN BOOTS (1987) • THE HOUSE THAT
JACK BUILT (1988) • THREE BLIND MICE (1990) • MARY, MARY (1993) •
THERE WAS A LITTLE GIRL (1994)

Other Novels

THE SENTRIES (1965) • WHERE THERE'S SMOKE • DOORS (1975) • GUNS
(1976) • ANOTHER PART OF THE CITY (1986) • DOWNTOWN (1991)

And as Evan Hunter

THE BLACKBOARD JUNGLE (1954) • SECOND ENDING (1956) • STRANGERS
WHEN WE MEET (1958) • A MATTER OF CONVICTION (1959) • MOTHERS
AND DAUGHTERS (1961) • BUDDWING (1964) • THE PAPER DRAGON
(1966) • A HORSE'S HEAD (1967) • LAST SUMMER (1968) • SONS (1969) •
NOBODY KNEW THEY WERE THERE (1971) • EVERY LITTLE CROOK AND
NANNY (1972) • COME WINTER (1973) • STREETS OF GOLD (1974) • THE
CHISHOLMS (1976) • LOVE, DAD (1981) • FAR FROM THE SEA (1983) •
LIZZIE (1984) • CRIMINAL CONVERSATION (1994) • PRIVILEGED
CONVERSATION (1996)

Short Story Collections

HAPPY NEW YEAR, HERBIE (1963) • THE EASTER MAN (1972)

Children's Books

FIND THE FEATHERED SERPENT (1952) • THE REMARKABLE HARRY (1959) • THE WONDERFUL BUTTON (1961) • ME AND MR STENNER (1976)

Screenplays

STRANGERS WHEN WE MEET (1959) • THE BIRDS (1962) • FUZZ (1972) • WALK PROUD (1979)

Teleplays

THE CHISHOLMS (1979) • THE LEGEND OF WALKS FAR WOMEN (1980) • DREAM WEST (1986)

This is for Charlotte and Dick Condon

The city in these pages is imaginary.
The people, the places are all fictitious.
Only the police routine is based on established
investigatory technique.

Detective Steve Carella wasn't sure he had heard the man correctly. This was not what a bereaved husband was supposed to say when his wife lay disemboweled on the bedroom floor in a pool of her own blood. The man was still wearing overcoat and homburg, muffler and gloves. He stood near the telephone on the night table, a tall man with a narrow face, the vertical plane of which was dramatically broken by a well-groomed gray mustache that matched the graying hair at his temples. His eyes were clear and blue and distinctly free of pain or grief. As if to make certain Carella had understood him, he repeated a fragment of his earlier statement, giving it even more emphasis this time around.

'*Very* glad she's dead,' he said.

'Sir,' Carella said, 'I'm sure I don't have to tell you . . .'

'That's right,' the man said, 'you don't have to tell me. It happens I'm a criminal lawyer. I am well aware of my rights, and fully cognizant of the fact that anything I tell you of my own free will may later be used against me. I repeat that my wife was a no-good bitch, and I'm delighted someone killed her.'

Carella nodded, opened his pad, glanced at it, and said, 'Are you the man who notified the police?'

'I am.'

'Then your name is Gerald Fletcher.'

'That's correct.'

'Your wife's name, Mr Fletcher?'

'Sarah. Sarah Fletcher.'

'Want to tell me what happened?'

'I got home about fifteen minutes ago. I called to my wife from the front door, and got no answer. I came here into the bedroom and found her dead on the floor. I immediately called the police.'

'Was the room in this condition when you came in?'

'It was.'

'Touch anything?'

'Nothing. I haven't moved from this spot since I placed the call.'

'Anybody in here when you came in?'

'Not a soul. Except my wife, of course.'

'And you say you got home about fifteen minutes ago?'

'More or less. You can check it with the elevator operator who took me up.'

Carella looked at his watch. 'That would have been ten-thirty or thereabouts.'

'Yes.'

'And you called the police at . . .' Carella consulted the open notebook. 'Ten thirty-four. Is that right?'

'I didn't look at my watch, but I expect that's close enough.'

'Well, the call was logged at . . .'

'Ten thirty-four is close enough.'

'Is that your suitcase in the entrance hallway?'

'It is.'

'Just returning home from a trip?'

'I was on the Coast for three days.'

'Where?'

'Los Angeles.'

'Doing what?'

'An associate of mine needed advice on a brief he's preparing.'

'What time did your plane get in?'

'Nine forty-five. I claimed my bag, caught a taxi, and came directly home.'

'And got here about ten-thirty, right?'

'That's right. For the third time.'

'Sir?'

'You've already ascertained the fact three times. If there remains any doubt in your mind, let me reiterate that I got here at ten-thirty, found my wife dead, and called the police at ten thirty-four.'

'Yes, sir, I've got that.'

'What's your name?' Fletcher asked suddenly.

'Carella. Detective Steve Carella.'

'I'll remember that.'

'Please do.'

While Fletcher was remembering Carella's name; and while the police photographer was doing his macabre little jig around the body, flashbulbs popping, death being recorded on Polaroid film for instant verification, pull, wait fifteen seconds, beep, rip, examine the picture to make sure the lady looks good in the rushes, or as good as any lady *can* look with her belly wide open and her intestines spilling onto a rug; and while two Homicide cops named Monoghan and Monroe beefed about being called away from their homes on a cold night in December, two weeks before Christmas; and while Detective Bert Kling was downstairs talking to the elevator operator and the doorman in an attempt to ascertain the *exact* hour Mr Gerald Fletcher had pulled up in a taxicab and entered the apartment building on Silvermine Oval and gone up in the elevator to find his once-beautiful wife, Sarah, spread amoeba-like in ugly death on the bedroom rug; while all this was happening, a laboratory technician named Marshall Davies was in the kitchen of the apartment, occupying himself with busy work while he waited for the Medical Examiner to pronounce the lady dead and state the probable cause (as if it took a genius to determine that someone had ripped her open with a switchblade knife), at which time Davies would go into the bedroom and with delicate care remove the knife protruding from the blood and slime of the lady's guts in an attempt to salvage some good latent prints from the handle of the murder weapon.

Davies was a new technician, but an observant one, and the first thing he noticed in the kitchen was that the window was wide open, not exactly usual for a December night when the temperature outside hovered at twelve degrees Fahrenheit, not to mention Centigrade. Davies leaned over the sink and further noticed that the window opened onto a fire escape on the rear of the building. Whereas he was paid only to examine the superficial aspects of any criminal act – such as glass shards in a victim's eyeball, or shotgun pellets in the chest, or, as in the case of the lady in the other room, a knife in the belly – he could not resist speculating that perhaps someone, some intruder, had climbed up the fire escape and into the kitchen, after which he had proceeded to the bedroom, where he'd done the lady in.

Since there was a big muddy footprint in the kitchen sink and another one on the floor near the sink, and several others fading in intensity as they traveled inexorably across the waxed kitchen floor to the door that led to the living room, Davies surmised he was onto something hot. Wasn't it entirely possible that an intruder *had* climbed over the windowsill and into the sink and walked across the room, bearing the switchblade knife that had later been pulled viciously across the lady's belly from left to right, like a rip-top cellophane tab, opening her as effortlessly as it would have a package of cigarettes?

Davies stopped speculating, and photographed the footprint in the sink and the ones on the floor. Then, because the Assistant ME was still fussing around with the corpse (Death by stab wound, Davies thought impatiently; evisceration, for Christ's sake!) and seemed reluctant to commit himself without perhaps first calling his superior officer or his mother (Say, we've got a tough one here, lady's belly ripped open with a knife, got any idea what might have caused death?), Davies climbed out onto the fire escape and dusted the lower edge of the window, which the intruder would have had to grab in order to open the window, and then for good measure dusted the iron railings of the ladder leading up to the fire escape.

Now, if the ME ever got through with the goddamn body, and if there were any latent prints on the handle of the knife, the boys of the 87th would be halfway home, thanks to Marshall Davies.

He felt pretty good.

Detective Bert Kling felt pretty lousy.

His condition, he kept telling himself, had nothing to do with the fact that Cindy Forrest had broken their engagement three weeks before. To begin with, it had never been a proper engagement, and a person certainly couldn't go around mourning something that had never truly existed. Besides, Cindy had made it abundantly clear that, whereas they had enjoyed some very good times together, and whereas she would always think upon him fondly and recall with great pleasure the days and months (yea, even years) they had spent together pretending they were in love, she had nonetheless met a very attractive young man who was a practicing psychiatrist at Buenavista Hospital, where she was doing her internship, and seeing as how they shared identical interests, and seeing as how he was quite ready to get married whereas Kling seemed to be married to a .38 Detective's Special, a scarred wooden desk, and a detention cage, Cindy felt it might be best to terminate their relationship immediately rather than court the possibility of trauma induced by slow and painful withdrawal.

That had been three weeks ago, and he had not seen nor called Cindy since, and the pain of the breakup was equaled only by the pain of the bursitis in his right shoulder, despite the fact that he was wearing a copper bracelet on his wrist. The bracelet had been given to him by none other than Meyer Meyer, whom no one would have dreamed of as a superstitious man given to beliefs in ridiculous claims. The bracelet was supposed to begin working in ten days (Well, maybe two weeks, Meyer had said, hedging) and Kling had been wearing it for eleven days now, with no relief for the bursitis, but with a noticeable green stain around his wrist just below the bracelet. Hope springs eternal. Somewhere in his race memory, there lurked a hulking ape-like creature rubbing animal teeth by a fire, praying in grunts for a splendid hunt on the morrow. Somewhere also in his race memory, though not as far back, was the image of Cindy Forrest naked in his arms, and the concomitant fantasy that she would call to say she'd made a terrible mistake and was ready to drop her psychiatrist pal. No Women's Lib man he, Kling nonetheless felt it perfectly all right for Cindy to take the initiative in re-establishing their relationship; it was she, after all, who had taken the first and final step toward ending it. Meanwhile, his bursitis hurt like hell and the elevator operator was not one of those bright snappy young men on the way up (Kling winced; he hated puns even when he made them himself), but rather a stupid clod who had difficulty remembering his own name. Kling went over the same tired ground yet another time.

'Do you know Mr Fletcher by sight?' he asked.

'Oh, yeah,' the elevator operator said.

'What does he look like?'

'Oh, you know, he calls me Max.'

'Yes, Max, but . . .'

'"Hello, Max," he says, "How are you, Max?" I say, "Hello there, Mr Fletcher, nice day today, huh?"'

'Could you describe him for me, please?'

'He's nice and handsome.'

'What color are his eyes?'

'Brown? Blue? Something like that.'

'How tall is he?'

'Tall.'

'Taller than you?'

'Oh, sure.'

'Taller than me?'

'Oh, no. About the same. Mr Fletcher is about the same.'

'What color hair does he have?'

'White.'

'White? Do you mean gray?'

'White, gray, something like that.'

'Which was it, Max, would you remember?'

'Oh, something like that. Ask Phil. He knows. He's good on times and things like that.'

Phil was the doorman. He was very good on times and things like that. He was also a garrulous lonely old man who welcomed the opportunity to be in a cops-and-robbers documentary film. Kling could not disabuse Phil of the notion that this was a *real* investigation; there was a dead lady upstairs and someone had brought about her present condition, and it was the desire of the police to bring that person to justice, ta-ra.

'Oh, yeah, yeah,' Phil said, 'terrible the way things are getting in this city, ain't it? Even when I was a kid, things wasn't this terrible. I was born over on the South Side, you know, in a neighborhood where if you wore shoes you were considered a sissy. We were all the time fighting with the wop gangs, you know? We used to drop things down on them from the rooftops. Bricks, eggs, scrap iron, a toaster one time – yeah, I swear to God, we once threw my mother's old toaster off the roof, *bang*, it hit one of them wops right on the head, bad place to hit a wop, of course, never does him no damage there. What I'm saying, though, is it never was so bad like it is now. Even when we were beating up the wops all the time, and them vice versa, it was fun, you know what I mean? I mean, it was *fun* in those days. Nowadays, what happens? Nowadays, you step in the elevator, there's some crazy dope fiend, he shoves a gun under your nose and says he'll blow your head off it you don't give him all your money. That happened to Dr Haskins, you think I'm kidding? He's coming home three o'clock in the morning, he goes in the elevator and Max is out taking a leak, so it's on self-service. Only there's a guy in the elevator, God knows how he even got in the building, probably came down from the roof, they jump rooftops like mountain goats, them dope fiends, and he sticks the gun right up under Dr Haskins' nose, right here, right pointing up his nostrils, for Christ's sake, and he says, Give me all your money and also whatever dope you got in that bag. So Dr Haskins figures What the hell, I'm going to get killed here for a lousy forty dollars and two vials of cocaine, here take it, good riddance. So he gives the guy what he wants, and you know what the guy does, anyway? He beats up Dr Haskins. They had to take him to the hospital with seven stitches, the son of a bitch split his forehead open with the butt of the pistol, he pistol-whipped him, you know? What kind of thing is that, huh? This city stinks, and especially this neighborhood. I can remember this neighborhood when you could come home three, four, five, even six o'clock in the morning, who cared what time you came home; you could be wearing a tuxedo and a mink coat, who cared what you were wearing, your jewels, your diamond cuff links, nobody bothered you. Try that today. Try walking down the street after dark without a Doberman pinscher on a leash, see how far you get. They smell you coming, these dope fiends, they leap out at you from doorways. We had a lot of burglaries in this building, all dope fiends. They come down from the roof, you know? We must've fixed that lock on the roof door a hundred times, what difference does it make? They're all experts, as soon as we fix it, *boom*, it's busted open again. Or they come up the fire escapes, who can stop them? Next thing you know, they're in some apartment stealing the whole place, you're lucky if they leave your false teeth in the glass. I don't know what this city's coming to, I swear to God. It's disgraceful.'

'What about Mr Fletcher?' Kling asked.

'What about him? He's a decent man, a lawyer. He comes home, and what does he find? He finds his wife dead on the floor, probably killed by some crazy dope fiend. Is that a way to live? Who needs it? You can't even go in your own bedroom without somebody jumping on you? What kind of thing is that?'

'When did Mr Fletcher come home tonight?'

'About ten-thirty,' Phil said.

'Are you sure of the time?'

'Positive. You know how I remember? There's Mrs Horowitz, she lives in 12C, she either doesn't have an alarm clock, or else she doesn't know how to set the alarm since her husband passed away two years ago. So every night she calls down to ask me the correct time, and to say would the day-man please call her at such and such a time in the morning, to wake her up. This ain't a hotel, but what the hell, an old woman asks a simple favor, you're supposed to refuse it?

Besides, she's very generous at Christmas, which ain't too far away, huh? So tonight, she calls down and says, "What's the correct time, Phil?" and I look at my watch and tell her it's ten-thirty, and just then Mr Fletcher pulls up in a taxicab. Mrs Horowitz says will I please ask the day-man to wake her up at seven-thirty, and I tell her I will and then go to the curb to carry Mr Fletcher's bag in. That's how I remember exactly what time it was.'

'Did Mr Fletcher go directly upstairs?'

'Directly,' Phil said. 'Why? Where would he go? For a walk in this neighborhood at ten-thirty in the night? That's like taking a walk off a gangplank.'

'Well, thanks a lot,' Kling said.

'Don't mention it,' Phil said. 'They shot another movie around here one time.'

Back at the ranch, they weren't shooting a movie. They were standing in an informal triangle around Gerald Fletcher, and raising their eyebrows at the answers he gave them. The three points of the triangle were Detective-Lieutenant Peter Byrnes and Detectives Meyer and Carella. Fletcher sat in a chair with his arms crossed over his chest. He was still wearing homburg, muffler, overcoat, and gloves, as if he expected to be called outdoors at any moment and wanted to be fully prepared for the inclement weather. The interrogation was being conducted in a windowless cubicle euphemistically labeled on its frosted glass door INTERROGATION ROOM. Opulently furnished in Institutional Wood, circa 1919, the room sported a long table, two straight-backed chairs, and a framed mirror. The mirror hung on a wall opposite the table. It was (heh-heh) a one-way mirror, which meant that on *this* side you saw your own reflection when you looked into the glass, but if you were standing on the *other* side, you could look into the room and observe all sorts of criminal behavior while

crime**masterworks**

Ed McBain

Sadie When
She Died

ORION

First published in 1972

This edition published in Great Britain in 2003 by Orion Books
an imprint of The Orion Publishing Group
Orion House, 5 Upper St Martin's Lane, London, WC2H 9EA

Copyright © 1972 by Evan Hunter
Copyright © renewed 2000 by Evan Hunter

A CIP catalogue record for this book
is available from the British Library

ISBN 0 75285 615 4

Typeset at SetSystems Ltd, Saffron Walden, Essex

Printed and bound in Great Britain by
Clays Ltd, St Ives plc

remaining unseen yourself; devious are the ways of law enforcers the world over. Devious, too, are the ways of criminals; there was not a single criminal in the entire city who did not recognize a one-way mirror the minute he laid eyes upon it. Quite often, in fact, criminals with a comic flair had been known to approach the mirror, place a thumb to the nose, and waggle the fingers of the hand as a gesture of esteem and affection to the eavesdropping cops on the other side of the glass. In such ways were mutual respect and admiration built between the men who broke the law and the men who tried to uphold it. Crime does not pay – but it doesn't hurt to have a few laughs along the way, as Euripides once remarked.

The cops standing in their loose triangle around Gerald Fletcher were amazed but not too terribly amused by his honesty, or, to be more exact, his downright brutal frankness. It was one thing to discuss the death of one's spouse without frills or furbelows; it was quite another to court lifelong imprisonment in a state penitentiary. Gerald Fletcher seemed to be doing precisely that.

'I hated her guts,' he said, and Meyer raised his eyebrows and glanced at Byrnes, who in turn raised his eyebrows and glanced at Carella, who was facing the one-way mirror and had the opportunity of witnessing his own reflection raising *its* eyebrows.

'Mr Fletcher,' Byrnes said, 'I know you understand your rights, as we explained them to you . . .'

'I understood them long before you explained them,' Fletcher said.

'And I know you've chosen to answer our questions without an attorney present . . .'

'I *am* an attorney.'

'What I meant . . .'

'I know what you meant. Yes, I'm willing to answer any and all questions without counsel.'

'I *still* feel I must warn you that a woman has been murdered . . .'

'Yes, my dear, wonderful wife,' Fletcher said sarcastically.

'Which is a serious crime . . .'

'Which, among felonies, may very well be the choicest of the lot,' Fletcher said.

'Yes,' Byrnes said. He was not an articulate man, but he felt somewhat tongue-tied in Fletcher's presence. Bullet-headed, hair turning from iron-gray to ice-white (slight bald spot beginning to show at the back), blue-eyed, built like a compact linebacker for the Minnesota Vikings, Byrnes straightened the knot in his tie, cleared his throat, and looked to his colleagues for support. Both Meyer and Carella were watching their shoelaces.

'Well, look,' Byrnes said, 'if *you* understand what you're doing, go right ahead. We warned you.'

'Indeed you *have* warned me. Repeatedly. I can't imagine why,' Fletcher said, 'since I don't feel myself to be in any particular danger. My wife is dead, someone killed the bitch. But it was not me.'

'Well, it's nice to have your assurance of that, Mr Fletcher, but your assurance alone doesn't necessarily still our doubts,' Carella said, hearing the words and wondering where the hell they were coming from. He was, he realized, trying to impress Fletcher, trying to ward off the man's obvious condescension by courting his acceptance. Look at me, he was pleading, listen to me. I'm not just a dumb bull, I'm a man of sensitivity and intelligence, able to understand your vocabulary, your sarcasm, and even your vituperative wit. Half-sitting upon, half-leaning against the scarred wooden table, a tall athletic-looking man with straight brown hair, brown eyes curiously slanted downwards, Carella folded his arms across his chest in unconscious imitation of Fletcher. The moment he realized what he was doing, he uncrossed his arms at once, and stared intently at Fletcher, waiting for an answer. Fletcher stared intently back.

'Well?' Carella said.

'Well what, Detective Carella?'

'Well, what do you have to say?'

'About what?'

'How do we know it *wasn't* you who stabbed her?'

'To begin with,' Fletcher said, 'there were signs of forcible entry in the kitchen and hasty departure in the bedroom – witness the wide-open window in the aforementioned room, and the shattered window in the latter. The drawers in the dining-room sideboard were open . . .'

'You're a very observant person,' Meyer said suddenly. 'Did you notice all this in the four minutes it took you to enter the apartment and call the police?'

'It's my *job* to be an observant person,' Fletcher said, 'but to answer your question, no. I noticed all this *after* I had spoken to Detective Carella here, and *while* he was on the phone reporting to your lieutenant. I might add that I've lived in that apartment on Silvermine Oval for the past twelve years, and that it doesn't take a particularly sharp-eyed man to notice that a bedroom window is smashed or a kitchen window open. Nor does it take a sleuth to realize that the family silver has been pilfered – especially when there are several serving spoons, soup ladles, and butter knives scattered on the bedroom floor beneath the shattered window. Have you checked the alleyway below the window? You're liable to find your murderer still lying there.'

'Your apartment is on the second floor, Mr Fletcher,' Meyer said.

'Which is why I suggested he might still be there,' Fletcher answered. 'Nursing a broken leg or a fractured skull.'

'In all my years of experience,' Meyer said, and Carella suddenly realized that *he*, too, was trying to impress Fletcher,

'I have never known a criminal to jump out a window on the second floor of a building.' (Carella was surprised he hadn't used the word 'defenestrate.')

'*This* criminal may have had good reason for imprudent action,' Fletcher said. 'He had just killed a woman, probably after coming upon her unexpectedly in an apartment he thought was empty. He had heard someone opening the front door, and had realized he could not leave the apartment the way he'd come in, the kitchen being too close to the entrance. He undoubtedly figured he would rather risk a broken leg than the penitentiary for life. How does *that* portrait compare to those of other Criminals You Have Known?'

'I've known *lots* of criminals,' Meyer said inanely, 'and some of them are too smart for their own damn good.' He felt idiotic even as he delivered his little preachment, but Fletcher had a way of making a man feel like a cretin. Meyer ran his hand self-consciously over his bald pate, his eyes avoiding the glances of Carella and Byrnes. Somehow, he felt he had let them all down. Somehow, a rapier thrust had been called for, and he had delivered only a puny mumbletypeg penknife flip. 'What about that knife, Mr Fletcher?' he said. 'Ever see it before?'

'Never.'

'It doesn't happen to be *your* knife, does it?' Carella asked.

'It does not.'

'Did your wife say anything to you when you entered the bedroom?'

'My wife was dead when I entered the bedroom.'

'You're sure of that?'

'I'm positive of it.'

'All right, Mr Fletcher,' Byrnes said abruptly. 'You want to wait outside, please?'

'Certainly,' Fletcher said, and rose, and left the room. The three detectives stood in silence for a respectable number of minutes. Then Byrnes said, 'What do you think?'

'I think he did it,' Carella said.

'What makes you think so?'

'Let me revise that.'

'Go ahead, revise it.'

'I think he *could* have done it.'

'Even with all those signs of a burglary?'

'*Especially* with all those signs.'

'Spell it out, Steve.'

'He could have come home, found his wife stabbed – but not fatally – and finished her off by yanking the knife across her belly. The ME's report says that death was probably instantaneous, either caused by severance of the abdominal aorta, or reflex shock, or both. Fletcher had four minutes when all he needed was maybe four *seconds*.'

'It's possible,' Meyer said.

'Or maybe I just don't like the son of a bitch,' Carella added.

'Let's see what the lab comes up with,' Byrnes said.

There were good fingerprints on the kitchen window sash, and on the silver drawer of the dining-room sideboard. There were good prints on some of the pieces of silver scattered on the floor near the smashed bedroom window. More important, although most of the prints on the handle of the switchblade knife were smeared, some of them were very good indeed. All of the prints matched; they had all been left by the same person.

Gerald Fletcher graciously allowed the police to take his fingerprints, which were then compared with those Marshall Davies had sent over from the police laboratory. The fingerprints on the window, the drawer, the silverware, and the knife did not match Gerald Fletcher's.

Which didn't mean a damn thing if he had been wearing his gloves when he finished her off.

2

On Monday morning, the sky above the River Harb was a cloudless blue. In Silvermine Park, young mothers were already pushing baby buggies, eager to take advantage of the unexpected December sunshine. The air was cold and sharp, but the sun was brilliant and it transformed the streets bordering the river into what they must have looked like at the turn of the century. A tugboat hooted, a gull shrieked and swooped low over the water, a woman tucked a blanket up under her baby's chin and cooed to him gently. Near the park railing, a patrolman stood with his hands behind his back, and idly stared out over the sun-dappled river.

Upstairs, in the second-floor rear apartment of 721 Silvermine Oval, a chalked outline on the bedroom floor was the only evidence that a woman had lain there in death the night before. Carella and Kling sidestepped the outline and moved to the shattered window. The lab boys had carefully lifted, packaged, and labeled the shards and slivers of glass, on the assumption that whoever had jumped through the window might have left bloodstains or clothing threads behind. Carella looked through the gaping irregular hole at the narrow alleyway below. There was a distance of perhaps twelve feet between this building and the one across from it. Conceivably, the intruder could have leaped across the shaftway, caught the windowsill on the opposite wall, and then boosted himself up into the apartment there. But this would have required premeditation and calculation, and if a person is going to make a trapeze leap for a windowsill, he doesn't dive through a closed window in haste and panic. The apartment across the way would have to be checked, of course; but the more probable likelihood was that the intruder had fallen to the pavement below.

'That's a long drop,' Kling said, peering over Carella's shoulder.

'How far do you figure?'

'Thirty feet. At least.'

'Got to break a leg taking a fall like that.'

'Maybe the guy's an acrobat.'

'You think he went through the window head first?'

'How else?'

'He might have broken the glass out first, and then gone through.'

'If he was about to go to all that trouble, why didn't he just *open* the damn thing?'

'Well, let's take a look,' Carella said.

They examined the latch, and they examined the sash.

'Okay to touch this?' Kling asked.

'Yeah, they're through with it.'

Kling grabbed both handles on the window frame and pulled up on them. 'Tough one,' he said.

'Try it again.'

Kling tugged again. 'I think it's stuck.'

'Probably painted shut,' Carella said.

'Maybe he *did* try to open it. Maybe he smashed it only when he realized it was stuck.'

'Yeah,' Carella said. 'And in a big hurry, too. Fletcher was opening the front door, maybe already in the apartment by then.'

'The guy probably swung his bag . . .'

'What bag?'

'Must've had a bag or something with him, don't you think? To put the loot in?'

'Probably. Though he couldn't have been too experienced.'

'What do you mean?'

'No gloves. Left prints all over the place. Got to be a beginner.'

'Even so, he'd have carried a bag. That's probably what he smashed the window with. Which might explain why there was silverware on the floor. He could've taken a wild swing when he realized the window was stuck, and maybe some of the stuff fell out of the bag.'

'Yeah, maybe,' Carella said.

'Then he probably climbed through the hole and dropped down feet first. That makes more sense than just *diving* through the thing, doesn't it? In fact, what he could've done, Steve, was drop the bag down first . . .'

'If he had a bag.'

'Every burglar in the world has a bag. Even beginners.'

'Well, maybe.'

'Well, *if* he had a bag, he could've dropped it down into the alley there, and *then* climbed out and hung from the sill before he jumped, you know what I mean? To make it a shorter distance.'

'I don't know if he had all that much time, Bert. Fletcher must've been in the apartment and heading for the bedroom by then.'

'Did Fletcher say anything about glass breaking? About hearing glass?'

'I don't remember asking him.'

'We'll have to ask him,' Kling said.

'Why? What difference does it make?'

'I don't know,' Kling said, and shrugged. 'But if the guy was still in the aparment when Fletcher came in . . .'

'Yeah?'

'Well, that cuts it very close, doesn't it?'

'He *must've* been here, Bert. He *had* to hear that front door opening. Otherwise, he'd have taken his good sweet time and gone out the kitchen window and down the fire escape, the way he'd come.'

'Yeah, that's right.' Kling nodded reflectively. 'Fletcher's lucky,' he said. 'The guy could just as easily have waited and stabbed him, too.'

'Let's take a look at that alley,' Carella said.

The woman looking through the ground-floor window saw only two big men in overcoats, poking around on the alley floor. Both men were hatless. One of them had brown hair and slanty Chinese eyes. The other one looked younger but no less menacing, a big blond tough with hardly nothing but peach fuzz on his face, the better to eat you, Grandma. She immediately went to the telephone and called the police.

In the alleyway, unaware of the woman who peered out at them from between the slats of her venetian blinds, Carella and Kling studied the concrete pavement, and then looked up at the shattered second-floor window of the Fletcher apartment.

'It's still a hell of a long drop,' Kling said.

'Looks even longer from down here.'

'Where do you suppose he'd have landed?'

'Right about where we're standing. Maybe a foot or so over,' Carella said, and looked at the ground.

'See anything?' Kling asked.

'No. I was just trying to figure something.'

'What?'

'Let's say he *did* land without breaking anything . . .'

'Well, he must've, Steve. Otherwise he'd still be laying here.'

'That's just my point. Even if he *didn't* break anything, I can't believe he just got up and walked away, can you?' He looked up at the window again. 'That's got to be at least forty feet, Bert.'

'Gets longer every minute,' Kling said. 'I still think it's no more than thirty, give or take.'

'Even so. A guy drops thirty feet . . .'

'If he hung from the windowsill first, you've got to subtract maybe ten feet from that figure.'

'Okay, so what do we say? A twenty-foot drop?'

'Give or take.'

'Guy drops twenty feet to a concrete pavement, doesn't break anything, gets up, dusts himself off, and runs the fifty-yard dash, right?' Carella shook his head. 'My guess is he stayed right where he was for a while. To at least catch his breath.'

'So?'

'So did Fletcher look out the window?'

'Why would he?'

'If your wife is dead on the floor with a knife in her, and the window is broken, wouldn't you naturally go to the window and look out? On the off chance you might spot the guy who killed her?'

'He was anxious to call the police,' Kling said.

'Why?'

'That's natural, Steve. If the guy's innocent, he's anxious to keep in the clear. He calls the police, he stays in the apartment . . .'

'I still think he did it,' Carella said.

'Don't make a federal case out of this,' Kling said. 'I personally would like nothing better than to kick Mr Fletcher in the balls, but let's concentrate on finding the guy whose fingerprints we've got, okay?'

'Yeah,' Carella said.

'I mean, Steve, be reasonable. If a guy's fingerprints are on the handle of a knife, and the knife is still in the goddamn victim . . .'

'*And* if the victim's husband realizes what a sweet setup he's stumbled into,' Carella said, 'wife laying on the floor with a knife in her, place broken into and burglarized, why *not* finish the job and hope the burglar will be blamed?'

'Sure,' Kling said. 'Prove it.'

'I can't,' Carella said. 'Not until we catch the burglar.'

'All right, so let's catch him. Where do you think he went after he dropped down here?'

'One of two ways,' Carella said. 'Either through the door there into the basement of the building. Or over the fence there at the other end of the alley.'

'Which way would you go?'

'If I'd just dropped twenty feet or more, I'd go home to my mother and cry.'

'I'd head for the door of the building. If I'd just dropped twenty feet, I wouldn't feel like climbing any fences.'

'Not with the terrible headache you'd probably have.'

The basement door suddenly opened. A red-faced patrolman was standing in the doorway with a .38 in his fist.

'All right, you guys, what's going on here?' he said.

'Oh, great,' Carella said.

Anyway, Marshall Davies had already done the work.

So while Carella and Kling went through the tedious routine of proving to a cop that they were cops themselves, Davies called the 87th Precinct and asked to talk to the detective who was handling the Fletcher homicide. Since *both* detectives who were handling the homicide were at that moment out handling it, or *trying* to, Davies agreed to talk to Detective Meyer instead.

'What've you got?' Meyer asked.

'I think I've got some fairly interesting information about the suspect.'

'Will I need a pencil?' Meyer asked.

'I don't think so. How much do you know about the case?'

'I've been filled in.'

'Then you know there were latent prints all over the apartment.'

'Yes. We've got the IS running a check on them now.'

'Maybe you'll get lucky.'

'Maybe,' Meyer said.

'Do you also know there were footprints in the kitchen?'

'No, I didn't know that.'

'Yes, a very good one in the sink, probably left there when he climbed through the window, and some middling-fair ones tracking across the kitchen floor to the dining room. I got some excellent pictures, and some very good blowups of the heel – for comparison purposes if the need arises later on.'

'Good,' Meyer said.

'But more important,' Davies said, 'I got a good walking picture from the footprints on the floor, and I think we can assume it was the man's usual gait, neither dawdling nor hurried.'

'How can you tell that?' Meyer asked.

'Well, if a man is walking slowly, the distance between his footprints is usually about twenty-seven inches. If he's running, his footprints will be about forty inches apart. Thirty-five inches apart is the average for fast walking.'

'How far apart were the prints you got?'

'Thirty-two inches. He was moving quickly, but he wasn't in a desperate hurry. The walking line, incidentally, was normal and not broken.'

'What does that mean?'

'Well, draw an imaginary line in the direction the suspect was walking, and that line should normally run along the inner edge of the heelprints. Fat people and pregnant ladies will often leave a broken walking line because they walk with their feet spread wider apart . . . to keep their balance.'

'But *this* walking line was normal,' Meyer said.

'Right,' Davies said.

'So our man is neither fat nor pregnant.'

'Right. Incidentally, it is a man. The size and type of the shoe, and also the angle of the foot indicate that clearly.'

'Okay, fine,' Meyer said. He did not thus far consider Davies' information valuable nor even terribly important. They had automatically assumed that anyone burglarizing an apartment would be a man and not a woman. Moreover, according to Carella's report on the size of the footprint in the sink, it had definitely been left by a man – unless a female Russian wrestler was loose in the precinct. Meyer yawned.

'Anyway, none of this is valuable nor even terribly import-ant,' Davies said, 'until we consider the rest of the data.'

'And what's that?' Meyer asked.

'Well, as you know, the bedroom window was smashed, and the Homicide men at the scene . . .'

'Monoghan and Monroe?'

'Yes, were speculating that the suspect had jumped through the window into the alley below. I didn't think it would hurt to go downstairs and see if I could get some meaningful pictures.'

'Did you get some meaningful pictures?'

'Yes, I got some pictures of where he must have landed – on both feet, incidentally – and I also got another walking picture and direction line. He moved toward the basement door and into the basement. That's not the important thing, however.'

'What is the important thing?' Meyer asked patiently.

'Our man is injured. And I think badly.'

'How do you know?'

'The walking picture downstairs is entirely different from the one in the kitchen. The footprints are the same, of course, no question but that the same person left them. But the walking line indicates that the person was leaning quite heavily on the left leg and dragging the right. There are, in fact, no *flat* footprints for the right foot, only scrape marks where the edges of the sole and heel were pulled along the concrete. I would suggest that whoever's handling the case put out a physician's bulletin. If this guy hasn't got a broken leg, I'll eat the pictures I took.'

A girl in a green coat was waiting in the lobby. Leaning against the wall, hands thrust deep into the slash pockets of the coat, she turned toward the basement door the instant it opened. Carella and Kling, followed by the red-faced patrolman (who was slightly *more* red-faced at the moment), came through the doorway and were starting for the street when the girl said, 'Excuse me, are you the detectives?'

'Yes?' Carella said.

'Hey, listen, I'm sorry,' the patrolman said. 'I just got transferred up here, you know, I ain't too familiar with all you guys.'

'That's okay,' Kling said.

'The super told me you were in the building,' the girl said.

'So, like excuse it, huh?' the patrolman said.

'Right, right,' Kling said, and waved him toward the front door.

'You're investigating the Fletcher murder, aren't you?' the girl said. She was quite soft-spoken, a tall girl with dark hair and large brown eyes that shifted alternately from one detective to the other, as though searching for the most receptive audience.

'How can we help you, miss?' Carella asked.

'I saw somebody in the basement last night,' she said. 'With blood on his clothes.'

Carella glanced at Kling, and immediately said, 'What time was this?'

'About a quarter to eleven,' the girl said.

'What were you doing in the basement?'

'My *clothes*,' the girl said, sounding surprised. 'That's where the washing machines are. I'm sorry, my name is Nora Simonov. I live here in the building.'

'So long, you guys,' the patrolman called from the front door. 'Excuse it, huh?'

'Right, right,' Kling said.

'I live on the fifth floor,' Nora said. 'Apartment 5A.'

'Tell us what happened, will you?' Carella said.

'I was sitting by the machine, watching the clothes tumble – which is simply *fascinating*, you know,' she said, and rolled her eyes and flashed a quick, surprising smile, 'when the door leading to the backyard opened. The door to the alley. You know the door I mean?'

'Yes,' Carella said.

'And this man came down the stairs. I don't even think he saw me. The machines are sort of off to the side, you know. He went straight for the steps at the other end, the ones that go up to the street. There are two flights of steps. One goes to the lobby, the other goes to the street. He went up to the street.'

'Was he anyone you recognized?'

'What do you mean?'

'From the building? Or the neighborhood?'

'No. I'd never seen him before last night.'

'Can you describe him?'

'Sure. He was about twenty-one, twenty-two years old, your height and weight, well, maybe a little bit shorter, five-ten or eleven. Brown hair.'

Kling was already writing. 'Notice the color of his eyes?' he said.

'No, I'm sorry.'

'Was he white or black?'

'White.'

'What was he wearing?'

'Dark trousers, high-topped sneakers, a poplin wind-breaker. With blood on the sleeve and on the front.'

'Which sleeve?'

'The right one.'

'Any hat?'

'No.'

'Was he carrying anything?'

'Yes. A small red bag. It looked like one of those bags the airlines give you.'

'Any scars, tattoos, marks?'

'Well, I couldn't say. He wasn't that close. And he went by in pretty much of a hurry, considering.'

'Considering *what*?' Carella asked.

'His leg. He was dragging his right leg. I think he was hurt pretty badly.'

'Would you recognize him if you saw him again?' Carella asked.

'In a minute,' Nora said.

What they had in mind, of course, was identification from a mug shot. What they had in mind was the possibility that the IS would come up with something positive on the fingerprints that had been sent downtown. What they all hoped was that maybe, just once, it would turn out to be a nice, easy one –

the Identification Section would send them the record of a known criminal, and they would pick him up without a fuss, and parade him in a squad-room lineup, from which Nora Simonov would pick him out as the man she had seen in the basement at 10:45 the night before, with blood on his clothes.

The IS reported that none of the fingerprints in their file matched the ones found in the apartment.

So the detectives sighed, and figured it was going to be a tough one after all (they are *all* tough ones, after all, they groaned, awash in a sea of self-pity), and did exactly what Marshall Davies had suggested: they sent out a bulletin to all of the city's doctors, asking them to report any leg fractures or sprains suffered by a white man in his early twenties, five feet ten or eleven inches tall, weighing approximately 180 pounds, brown hair, last seen wearing dark trousers, high-topped sneakers, and a poplin windbreaker with bloodstains on the front and on the right sleeve.

And, just to prove that cops can be as wrong as anyone else, it turned out to be a nice, easy one, after all.

The call came from a physician in Riverhead at 4:37 that afternoon, just as Carella was ready to go home.

'This is Dr Mendelsohn,' he said. 'I have your bulletin here, and I want to report treating a man who fits your description.'

'Where are you located, Dr Mendelsohn?' Carella asked.

'On Dover Plains Avenue. In Riverhead. 3461 Dover Plains.'

'When did you treat this man?'

'Early this morning. I have early office hours on Monday. It's my day at the hospital.'

'What did you treat him for?'

'A bad ankle sprain.'

'No fracture?'

'None. We X-rayed the leg here. It was quite swollen, and I suspected a fracture, of course, but it was merely a bad sprain. I taped it for him, and advised him to stay off it for a while.'

'Did he give you his name?'

'Yes. I have it right here.'

'May I have it, sir?'

'Ralph Corwin.'

'Any address?'

'894 Woodside.'

'In Riverhead?'

'Yes.'

'Thank you, Dr Mendelsohn,' Carella said.

'Not at all,' Mendelsohn said, and hung up.

Carella pulled the Riverhead telephone directory from the top drawer of his desk, and quickly flipped to the C's. He did not expect to find a listing for Ralph Corwin. A man would have to be a rank amateur to first burglarize an apartment without wearing gloves, then stab a woman to death, and then give his name when seeking treatment for an injury sustained in escaping from the murder apartment.

Ralph Corwin was apparently a rank amateur.

His name was in the phone book, and the address he'd given the doctor was as true as the day was long.

They kicked in the door without warning, fanning into the room, guns drawn.

The man on the bed was wearing only undershorts. His right ankle was taped. The bedsheets were soiled, and the stench of vomit in the close, hot room was overpowering.

'Are you Ralph Corwin?' Carella asked.

'Yes,' the man said. His face was drawn, the eyes squinched in pain.

'Police officers,' Carella said.

'What do you want?'

'We want to ask you some questions. Get dressed, Corwin.'

'There's nothing to ask,' he said, and turned his head into the pillow. 'I killed her.'

3

Ralph Corwin made his confession in the presence of two detectives of the 87th Squad, a police stenographer, an assistant district attorney, and a lawyer appointed by the Legal Aid Society. The man from the DA's office conducted the Q and A.

Q: What is your name, please?
A: Ralph Corwin.
Q: Where do you live, Mr Corwin?
A: 894 Woodside Avenue. In Riverhead.
Q: Will you relate to us, please, the events that took place on the night of December twelfth. That would be last night, Mr Corwin, Sunday, December twelfth.
A: Where do you want me to start?
Q: Did you enter a building at 721 Silvermine Oval?
A: I did.
Q: How did you enter the building?
A: First I went down the steps from the street, where the garbage cans were. I went in the basement, and through the basement and up the steps at the other end, into the backyard. Then I climbed up the fire escape.
Q: What time was this?
A: I went in the building at about ten o'clock.

Q: Ten P.M.?

A: Yes, ten P.M.

Q: What did you do then?

A: I went in an apartment.

Q: Which apartment?

A: Second-floor rear.

Q: Why did you go into the apartment?

A: To rip it off.

Q: To burglarize it?

A: Yes.

Q: Had you ever been in this building before?

A: No. I never done nothing like this in my life before. Never. I'm a junkie, that's true, but I never stole nothing in my life before this. Nor hurt nobody, either. I wouldn't have stole now except this girl I was living with left me, and I was desperate. She used to give me whatever bread I needed. But she left me. Friday. She just walked out.

Q: Which girl is that?

A: Do we have to drag her in? She's got nothing to do with it. She never done me no harm, I got no hard feelings toward her, even though she walked out. She was always good to me. I don't want to drag her name in this.

Q: You say you had never been in this building before?

A: Never.

Q: Why did you pick this particular apartment to enter?

A: It was the first one I saw without no lights inside. I figured there was nobody home.

Q: How did you get into the apartment?

A: The kitchen window was open a tiny crack. I squeezed my fingers under the bottom of it, and opened it all the way.

Q: Were you wearing gloves?

A: No.

Q: Why not?

A: I don't have no gloves. Gloves cost money. I'm a junkie.

Q: Weren't you afraid of leaving fingerprints?

A: I figured that was crap. For the movies, you know? For television. Anyway, I don't *have* no gloves, so what difference does it make?

Q: What did you do after you opened the window?

A: I stepped in the sink, and then down to the floor.

Q: Then what?

A: I had this little flashlight. So I used it to find my way across the kitchen to the dining room.

Q: Would you look at this photograph, please?

A: Yeah?

Q: Is this the kitchen you were in?

A: I don't know. It was dark. I guess it could be. I don't know.

Q: What did you do in the dining room?

A: I found where they kept the silverware, and I emptied the drawer and put the stuff in this airlines bag I had with me. I had to go to Chicago last month because my father died, so I went by plane, and I bought this little airlines bag. My girlfriend paid for me to fly out there. She was a great girl, I wish I could figure why she left. I wouldn't be in this trouble now, if she'd stayed, you know that? I never stole nothing in my life, nothing, I swear to God. And I never hurt nobody. I don't know what got into me. I must've been scared out of my wits. That's the only thing I can figure.

Q: Where did you go when you left the dining room?

A: I was looking for the bedroom.

Q: Was the flashlight on?

A: Yeah. It's just this little flashlight. A penlight is what they call them, A tiny little thing, you know? So you can have some light.

Q: Why were you looking for the bedroom?

A: I figured that's where people leave watches and rings, stuff like that. I was going to take whatever jewelry I could find and then get out. I'm not a pro, I was just hung up real bad and needed some bread to tide me over.

Q: Did you find the bedroom?

A: I found it.

Q: What happened?

A: There was a lady in bed. This was only like close to ten-thirty, you don't expect nobody to be asleep so early, you know what I mean? I thought the apartment was empty.

Q: But there was a woman in bed.

A: Yeah. She turned on the light the minute I stepped in the room.

Q: What did you do?

A: I had a knife in my pocket. I pulled it out.

Q: Why?

A: To scare her.

Q: Would you look at this knife, please?

A: Yeah, it's mine.

Q: This is the knife you took from your pocket?

A: Yeah. Yes.

Q: Did the woman say anything to you?

A: Yeah, it was almost comical. I mean, when I think back on it, it was comical, though at the time I was very scared. But it was like a movie, you know? Just like a movie. She looks at me and she says 'What are you doing here?' Which is funny, don't you think? I mean, what did she *think* I was doing there?

Q: Did you say anything to her?

A: I told her to keep quiet, that I wasn't going to hurt her.

Q: Then what?

A: She got out of bed. Not all the way, she just threw the covers back, and swung her legs over the side, you know? Sitting, you know? I didn't realize what was happening for a minute, and then I saw she was reaching for the phone. That's got to be crazy, right? A guy is standing there in your bedroom with a knife in his hand, so she reaches for the phone.

Q: What did you do?

A: I grabbed her hand before she could get it. I pulled her off the bed, away from the phone, you know? And I told her again that nobody was going to hurt her, that I was getting out of there right away, to just please calm down.

Q: You said that?

A: What?

Q: You asked her to calm down?

A: I don't know if those were the exact words, but I told her like to take it easy because I could see she was getting hysterical.

Q: Would you look at this photograph, please? Is this the bedroom you were in?

A: Yeah. There's the night table with the phone on it, and there's the window I went out. That's the room.

Q: What happened next?

A: She started to scream.

Q: What did you do when she screamed?

A: I told her to stop. I was beginning to panic by now. I mean, she was really yelling.

Q: Did she stop?

A: No.

Q: What did you do?

A: I stabbed her.

Q: Where did you stab her?

A: I don't know. It was a reflex. She was yelling, I was afraid the whole building would come down. I just . . . I just stuck the knife in her. I was very scared.

Q: Did you stab her in the chest?

A: No.

Q: Where?

A: The belly. Someplace in the belly.

Q: How many times did you stab her?

A: Once. She . . . she backed away from me, I'll never forget the look on her face. And she . . . she fell on the floor.

Q: Would you look at this photograph, please?

A: Oh, Jesus.

Q: Is that the woman you stabbed?

A: Oh, Jesus. Oh, Jesus, I didn't think . . . oh, Jesus.

Q: Is that the woman?

A: Yes. Yes, that's her. Yes.

Q: What happened next?

A: Can I have a drink of water?

Q: Get him a drink of water. You stabbed her, and she fell to the floor. What happened next?

A: There was . . .

Q: Yes?

A: There was somebody at the door. I heard the door opening. Then somebody came in.

Q: Came into the apartment?

A: Yes. And yelled her name.

Q: From the front door?

A: I guess. From someplace at the other end of the apartment.

Q: Called her name?

A: Yeah. He yelled, 'Sarah!' and when he got no answer, he yelled, 'Sarah, it's me, I'm home.'

Q: Then what?

A: I knew I was trapped. I couldn't go out the way I come in because this guy was home. So I ran past the . . . the woman where she was laying on the floor . . . Jesus . . . and I tried to open the window, but it was stuck. So I smashed it with the airlines bag and . . . I didn't know what to do . . . I was on the second floor, how was I going to get out? I threw the bag down first because I figured no matter what happened I was going to need bread for another fix, and then I climbed through the broken window – I cut my hand on a piece of glass – and I hung down from the sill, scared to let go, and finally I let go, I had to let go.

Q: Yes?

A: I must've dropped a mile, it felt like a mile. The minute I hit, I knew I busted something. I tried to get up, and I fell right down. My ankle was killing me, my hand was bleeding. I must've been in that alley ten, fifteen minutes, trying to stand up, falling down, trying again. I finally made it. I finally got out of that alley.

Q: Where did you go?

A: Through the basement and up to the street. The way I come in.

Q: And where did you go from there?

A: I took the subway home. To Riverhead. I turned on the radio right away to see if there was anything about . . . about what I done. But there wasn't. So I tried to go to sleep, but the ankle was very bad, and I needed a fix. I went to see Dr Mendelsohn in the morning because I figured it was like life or death, you know what I mean? If I couldn't get around, how was I going to make a connection?

Q: When did you visit Dr Mendelsohn?

A: Early. Nine o'clock. Nine A.M.

Q: Is he your family physician?

A: I never saw him before in my life. He's around the corner from where I live. That's the only reason I picked him, because he was close. He strapped up the ankle, but it didn't do no good. I *still* can't walk on it, I'm like a lousy cripple. I told him to bill me for it. I was going to pay him as soon as I got some bread. That's why I gave him my right name and address. I wasn't going to cheat him. I'm not that kind of person. I know that what I done is bad, but I'm not a bad person.

Q: When did you learn that Mrs Fletcher was dead?

A: I bought a newspaper on the way home from the doctor's. The story was in it. That's when I knew I killed her.

Q: You did not know until then?

A: I did not know how bad it was.

4

On Tuesday, December 14, which was the first of Carella's two days off that week, he received a call at home from Gerald Fletcher. He knew that no one in the squad room would have given his home number to a civilian, and he further knew that the number was unlisted in the Riverhead directory. Puzzled, he said, 'How'd you get my number, Mr Fletcher?'

'Friend of mine in the DA's office,' Fletcher said.

'Well, what can I do for you?' Carella asked. His voice, he realized, was something less than cordial.

'I'm sorry to bother you at home this way.'

'It *is* my day off,' Carella said, fully aware that he was being rude.

'I wanted to apologize for the other night,' Fletcher said.

'Oh?' Carella answered, surprised.

'I know I behaved badly. You men had a job to do, and I wasn't making it any easier for you. I've been trying to understand what provoked my attitude, and I can only think I must have been in shock. I disliked my wife, true, but finding her dead that way was probably more unnerving than I realized. I'm sorry if I caused any trouble.'

'No trouble at all,' Carella said. 'You've been informed, of course, that . . .'

'Yes, you caught the murderer.'

'Yes.'

'That was fast and admirable work, Detective Carella. And it only adds to the embarrassment I feel for having behaved so idiotically.'

'Well,' Carella said, and the line went silent.

'Please accept my apologies,' Fletcher said.

'Sure,' Carella said, beginning to feel embarrassed himself.

'I was wondering if you're free for lunch today.'

'Well,' Carella said, 'I was going to get some Christmas shopping done. My wife and I made out a list last night, and I thought . . .'

'Will you be coming downtown?'

'Yes, but . . .'

'Perhaps you could manage both.'

'Well, look, Mr Fletcher,' Carella said, 'I know you feel bad about the other night, but you said you're sorry and that's enough, believe me. It was nice of you to call, I realize it wasn't an easy thing to . . .'

'Why not meet me at The Golden Lion at one o'clock?' Fletcher said. 'Christmas shopping can be exhausting. You might welcome a break along about then.'

'Well . . . where's The Golden Lion?' Carella asked.

'On Juniper and High.'

'Downtown? Near the Criminal Courts Building?'

'Exactly. Do you know it?'

'I'll find it.'

'One o'clock then?' Fletcher said.

'Well, yeah, okay,' Carella said.

'Good, I'll look for you.'

Carella did not know why he went to see Sam Grossman at the Police Lab that afternoon. He told himself that he was going to be in the neighborhood, anyway, The Golden Lion being all the way downtown in the area bordered by the city's various courthouses. But this did not explain why he rushed through the not-unpleasant task of choosing a doll for his daughter, April, in order to get to Police Headquarters on High Street a full half hour before he was to meet Fletcher.

Grossman was hunched over a microscope when Carella walked in, but without opening his one closed eye, and without raising his head from the eyepiece, he said, 'Sit down, Steve, be with you in a minute.'

Grossman kept adjusting the focus and jotting notes on a pad near his right hand, never lifting his head. Carella was trying to puzzle out how Grossman had known it was he. The sound of his footfalls? The smell of his aftershave lotion? The faint aroma of his wife's perfume clinging to the shoulder of his overcoat? He had not, until this moment, been aware that Detective-Lieutenant Sam Grossman, he of the spectacles and sharp blue eyes, he of the craggy face and clipped no-nonsense voice, was in reality Sherlock Holmes of 221B Baker Street, who was capable of recognizing a man without looking at him. Grossman's remarkable trick occupied all of Carella's thoughts for the next five minutes. At the end of that time, Grossman looked up from the microscope, extended his hand, and said, 'What brings you to the eighth circle?'

'How'd you know it was me?'

'Huh?' Grossman said.

'I came into the room, and you never looked up, but you said, "Sit down, Steve, be right with you." How'd you know it was me without first *looking* at me?'

'Ah-ha,' Grossman said.

'No, come on, Sam, it's bugging the hell out of me.'

'Well, it's really quite simple,' Grossman said, grinning. 'You will notice that the time is now twenty-five minutes to one, and that the sun, having passed its zenith, is glancing obliquely through the bank of windows lining the laboratory wall, touching the clock ever so faintly and casting shadows the angle of which can easily be measured.'

'Mmm?' Carella said.

'Moreover, the specimen on this microscope slide is particularly light-sensitive, meaning that the slightest deviation of any ray you might care to name – X, ultraviolet, or infrared – could easily have caused recognizable changes on the slide while I was examining it. Couple this, Steve, with the temperature, which I believe is close to ten above zero, and the air pollution level, which is, as *usual* in this city, unsatisfactory, and you can understand how all this might account for immediate identification without visibility being a necessary factor.'

'Yeah?' Carella said.

'Exactly. There's one other important point, of course, and I think we should consider it, too, if we're to understand the complete picture. You wanted to know how I knew you had entered the laboratory and were approaching the worktable? To begin with, when I heard the door opening . . .'

'How'd you know it was *me*?'

'Well, here's the single *most* important element in the deductive process that led me to my inescapable conclusion . . .'

'Yes, *what*?'

'Marshall Davies saw you in the hall. He popped in just before you opened the door, to tell me you were coming.'

'You son of a bitch,' Carella said, and burst out laughing.

'How do you like the job he did for you guys?' Grossman asked.

'Beautiful,' Carella said.

'Practically handed it to you on a platter.'

'No question.'

'The Police Laboratory strikes again,' Grossman said. 'Pretty soon we'll be able to do without you guys entirely.'

'I know. That's why I came down to see you. I want to turn in my badge.'

'About time,' Grossman said. 'Why *did* you come down? Big case you want us to crack in record time?'

'Nothing more important than a couple of purse snatches on Culver Avenue.'

'Bring the victims in. We'll try to lift some latents from their backsides,' Grossman said.

'I don't think they'd like that,' Carella said.

'And why not? We would treat the ladies with great delicacy.'

'Oh, I don't think the *lady* would mind. But the *guy* whose purse was snatched . . .'

'You son of a bitch!' Grossman shouted, and both men began laughing hysterically.

'Seriously,' Carella said, laughing.

'Yes, yes, seriously,' Grossman said.

'Listen, I'm really trying to be serious here.'

'Yes, yes, of course.'

'I came down to thank you.'

'For what?' Grossman said, sobering immediately.

'I was about to go out on a limb. The stuff you got for us clinched the case and made an arrest possible. I wanted to thank you, that's all.'

'What kind of a limb, Steve?'

'I thought the husband did it.'

'Mmm?'

'Mmm.'

'Why!'

'No reason.' Carella paused. 'Sam,' he said, 'I *still* think he did it.'

'Is that why you're having lunch with him today?' Grossman asked.

'Now how the hell do you know *that?*' Carella said.

'Ah-ha,' Grossman answered. 'He was in Rollie Chabrier's office when he called you. I spoke to Rollie a little while after that, and . . .'

'Good day, sir,' Carella said. 'You're too much of a smart-ass for me.'

Most policemen in the city for which Carella worked did not very often eat in restaurants like The Golden Lion. They ate lunch at one or another of the greasy spoons in and around the precinct, where the meal was on the arm, tribute to Caesar. Or they grabbed a quick sandwich and a cup of coffee at their desks. On their own time, when they entertained wives or girl friends, they often dropped in on restaurants where they were known as cops, protesting demonstratively when the proprietor said, 'This is on the house,' but accepting the gratuity nonetheless. Not a single cop in the city considered the practice dishonest. They were underpaid and overworked and they were here to protect the average citizen against criminal attack. If some of those citizens were in a position to make the policeman's lot a bit more tolerable, why should they embarrass those persons by refusing a free meal graciously offered? Carella had never been inside The Golden Lion. A look at the menu posted on the window outside would have frightened him out of six months' pay.

The place was a faithful replica of the dining room of an English coach house, circa 1637. Huge oaken beams crossed the room several feet below the vaulted ceiling, binding together the rough white plastered walls. The tables were sturdy, covered with immaculate white cloths, sparkling with heavy silver. Here and there throughout the room there hung the portraits of Elizabethan gentlemen and ladies, white-laced collars and cuffs discreetly echoing the color of the walls, rich velvet robes or gowns adding muted touches of color to the pristine candlelit atmosphere. Gerald Fletcher's table was in a secluded corner of the restaurant. He rose as Carella approached, extended his hand, and immediately said, 'Glad you could make it. Sit down, won't you?'

Carella shook Fletcher's hand, and then sat. He felt extremely uncomfortable, nor could he tell whether his discomfort was caused by the room or the man with whom he was dining. The room was intimidating, true, brimming with lawyers discussing their most recent cases in voices best saved for juries. In their presence Carella felt somewhat like a numbers collector in the policy racket, picking up the work to deliver it to the higher-ups for processing and final disposition. The law was his life, but in the midst of lawyers he felt like a menial. The man sitting opposite him was a criminal lawyer, which was intimidating in itself. But he was something more than that, and it was this perhaps that made Carella feel awkward and clumsy in his presence. It did not matter whether or not Fletcher truly *was* cleverer than Carella, or more sophisticated, or better at his work, or handsomer, or more articulate – the truth was unimportant. Carella *felt* Fletcher was all of these things; the man's manner and bearing and attack (yes, it could be called nothing else) utterly convinced Carella that he was in the presence of a superior being, and this was as good as, if not more potent than, the actual truth.

'Would you care for a drink?' Fletcher asked.

'Well, are you having one?' Carella asked.

'Yes, I am.'

'I'll have a scotch and soda,' Carella said. He was not used to drinking at lunch. He *never* drank at lunch when he was on duty, and the next time he would drink at lunch in his own home would be on Christmas Day, when the family came to celebrate the holiday.

Fletcher signaled for the waiter. 'Have you ever been here before?' he asked Carella.

'No, never.'

'I thought you might have. It being so close to all the courts. You *do* spend a lot of time in court, don't you?'

'Yes, quite a bit,' Carella said.

'Ah,' Fletcher said to the waiter. 'A scotch and soda, please, and another whiskey sour for me.'

'Thank you, Mr Fletcher,' the waiter said, and padded off.

'I cannot tell you how impressed I was by the speed with which you people made your arrest,' Fletcher said.

'Well, we had a lot of help from the lab,' Carella said.

'Incredible, wasn't it? I'm talking about the man's carelessness. But then I understand from Rollie . . .' Fletcher paused. 'Rollie Chabrier, in the DA's office. I believe you know him.'

'Yes, I do.'

'He's the one who gave me your home number. I hope you won't think too badly of him for it.'

'No, no, quite all right,' Carella said.

'I called you directly from his office this morning. Quite coincidentally, he'll be prosecuting the case against Corwin.'

'Scotch and soda, sir?' the waiter asked rhetorically, and set the drink down before Carella. He put the second whiskey sour on the table before Fletcher and then said, 'Would you care to see menus now, Mr Fletcher?'

'In a bit,' Fletcher said.

'Thank you, sir,' the waiter answered, and went off again.

Fletcher raised his glass. 'Here's to a conviction,' he said.

Carella lifted his own glass. 'I don't expect Rollie'll have any trouble,' he said. 'It looks airtight to me.'

Both men drank. Fletcher dabbed his lips with a napkin and said, 'You never can tell these days. I practice criminal law, as you know, and I'm usually on the other side of the fence. You'd be surprised at the number of times we've won acquittal on cases that seemed cinches for the people.' He lifted his glass again. His eyes met Carella's. 'I hope you're

right, though,' he said. 'I hope this one *is* airtight.' He sipped
at the drink. 'Rollie was telling me . . .'

'Yes, you were starting to say . . .'

'Yes, that the man is a drug addict . . .'

'Yes . . .'

'Who'd never before burglarized an apartment.'

'That's right.'

'I must admit I feel a certain amount of sympathy for
him.'

'Do you?'

'Yes. If he's an addict he's automatically entitled to pity.
And when one considers that the woman he murdered was a
bitch like my wife . . .'

'Mr Fletcher . . .'

'Gerry, okay?'

'Well . . .'

'I know, I know. It isn't very kind of me to malign the
dead. I'm afraid you didn't know my wife, though, Mr
Carella. May I call you Steve?'

'Sure.'

'My enmity might be a bit more understandable if you
did. Still, I *shall* take your advice. She's dead, and no longer
capable of hurting me. So why be bitter? Shall we order,
Steve?'

The waiter came to the table. Fletcher suggested that
Carella try either the trout *au meunière* or the beef and kidney
pie, both of which were excellent. Carella ordered prime ribs,
medium rare, and a mug of beer. As the men ate and talked,
something began happening. Or at least Carella *thought*
something was happening; he would never be quite sure. Nor
would he ever try to explain the experience to anyone because
the conversation with Fletcher seemed on the surface to be
routine chatter about such unrelated matters as conditions in
the city, the approaching holidays, several recent motion

pictures, the effectiveness of the copper bracelet Meyer had given Kling, the University of Wisconsin (where Fletcher had gone to law school), the letters Carella's children had written and were still writing daily to Santa Claus, the quality of the beef, and the virtues of ale as compared to beer. But rushing through this inane, polite, and really quite pointless discussion was an undercurrent that caused excitement, fear, and apprehension. As they spoke, Carella knew with renewed dizzying certainty that Gerald Fletcher had killed his wife. Without ever being told so, he knew it. Without the murder ever being mentioned again, he knew it. *This* was why Fletcher had called this morning, *this* was why Fletcher had invited him to lunch, *this* was why he prattled on endlessly while every contradictory move of his body, every hand gesture, every facial expression signaled, indicated, transmitted on an almost extrasensory level that he *knew* Carella suspected him of the murder, and was here to tell Carella (without telling him) that, Yes, you stupid cop bastard, yes, I killed my wife. However much the evidence may point to another man, however many confessions you get, I killed the bitch, and I'm glad I killed her.

And there isn't a goddamn thing you can do about it.

5

Ralph Corwin was being held before trial in the city's oldest prison, known to law enforcers and law breakers alike as 'Calcutta.' How Calcutta had evolved from Municipal House of Detention, Male Offenders was anybody's guess. The automatic reference, one might have thought, would be to 'The Black Hole,' but Calcutta was not bad as prisons went; there were certainly less hanging-suicides among *its* inmates than there were at several of the city's other fine establishments. The building itself was old, but built at a time when masons knew how to handle bricks (and, more important, *cared* how they were handled) and so it had withstood the onslaught of time and weather, yielding only to the city's soot, which covered the rust-red bricks like a malevolent black jungle fungus. Inside the buildings, the walls and corridors were clean, the cells small but sanitary, the recreational facilities (Ping-Pong, television, and, in the open yard outside, handball) adequate, and the guards about as dedicated as those to be found anywhere – which is to say they were brutal, sadistic, moronic clods. Ralph Corwin was being kept in a wing of the building reserved for heavy felony offenders; his cell block at the moment was occupied by himself, a gentleman who had starved his six-year-old son to death in the basement of his Calm's Point house, another gentleman who had set fire to a synagogue in Majesta, and a third member of the criminal elite who had shot and blinded a gas-station attendant during a holdup in Bethtown. The wounded attendant had rushed out into the highway gushing blood from his shattered face and, because he could not see, was knocked down and killed by a two-ton trailer truck. As the old gag goes, however, he wouldn't have died if he hadn't been shot first. Corwin's cell was at the end of the row, and Carella found him there that Wednesday morning sitting on the lower bunk, hands clasped between his knees, head bent as though in prayer. It had been necessary to get permission for the visit from both the district attorney's office and Corwin's lawyer, neither of whom, apparently, felt that allowing Carella to talk to the prisoner would be harmful to the case. Corwin was expecting him. He lifted his head as soon as he heard approaching footsteps, and then rose from the bunk as the turnkey opened the cell door.

'How are you?' Carella said, and extended his hand. Corwin took it, shook it briefly, and then said, 'I was wondering which one you'd be. I got your names mixed up, you and the blond cop, I couldn't remember which was which. Anyway, now I know. You're Carella.'

'Yes.'

'What'd you want to see me about?'

'I wanted to ask you some questions.'

'My lawyer says . . .'

'I spoke to your lawyer, he knows . . .'

'Yeah, but he says I'm not supposed to add anything to what I already said. He wanted to *be* here, in fact, but I told him I could take care of myself. I don't even *like* that guy. Did you ever meet that guy? He's this little fink with glasses, he's like a goddamn cockroach.'

'Why don't you ask for another lawyer?'

'Can I do that?'

'Sure.'

'Who do I ask?'

'The Legal Aid Society.'

'Can *you* do that for me? Can you give them a call and tell them . . .'

'I'd rather not.'

'Why?' Corwin said, and studied Carella suspiciously.

'I don't want to do anything that might be considered prejudicial to the case.'

'Whose case? Mine or the DA's?'

'Either one. I'm not familiar enough with what the Court might consider . . .'

'Okay, so how do *I* call the Legal Aid?'

'Ask one of the officers here. Or simply tell your lawyer. I'm sure if you explain your feelings to him, he would have no objection to dropping out. Would *you* want to defend someone who didn't like you?'

'Yeah, well,' Corwin said, and shrugged. 'I don't want to hurt his feelings. He's a little cockroach, but what the hell.'

'You've got a lot at stake here, Corwin.'

'That's just the point. What the hell difference does it make?'

'What do you mean?'

'I killed her. So what does it matter *who* the lawyer is? Nobody's going to save me. You got it all in black and white.'

Corwin's eyelid was twitching. He wrung his hands together, sat on the bunk again, and said, 'I got to hold my hands together. I got to squeeze them together, otherwise I'm afraid I'll shake myself to pieces, you know what I mean?'

'How bad has it been?'

'Cold turkey's never good, and it's worse when you can't yell. Every time I yell, that son of a bitch in the next cell tells me to shut up, the one who put his own kid in the basement. He scares me. Did you get a look at him? He must weigh two hundred and fifty pounds. Can you imagine a guy like that chaining his own kid in the basement? And not giving him anything to eat? What makes people do things like that?'

'I don't know,' Carella said. 'Have they given you any medication?'

'No. They said this ain't a hospital. Which I *know* it ain't, right? So I asked my cockroach lawyer to get me transferred to the Narcotics Service at Buenavista, and he said the prison authorities would have to make tests before they could transfer me there as a bona-fide addict, and he said that might take a couple of days. So in a couple of days I won't *be* a fuckin' bona-fide addict anymore, because by then I'll vomit up my guts and kick it cold turkey, so what kind of sense does that make? I don't understand rules. I swear to God, I really don't understand rules. That's one thing about junk. It makes you forget all the bullshit rules. You stick a needle in your arm, all the rules vanish. Man, I *hate* rules.'

'You feel like answering some questions?' Carella said.

'I feel like dropping dead is what I feel like.'

'If you'd rather I came back another . . .'

'No, no, go ahead. What do you want to know?'

'I want to know exactly how you stabbed Sarah Fletcher.'

Corwin squeezed his hands tightly together. He wet his lips, abruptly leaned forward as though fighting a sudden cramp, and said, 'How do you *think* you stab somebody? You stick a knife in her, that's how.'

'Where?'

'In the belly.'

'Left-hand side of the body?'

'Yes. I guess so. I'm right-handed, and she was facing me, so I guess that's where I stabbed her. Yes.'

'Then what?'

'What do you mean?'

'What did you do then?'

'I . . . you know, I think I must've let go of the knife. I think I was so surprised I stabbed her that I let go of it, you know? I must've let go, don't you think? Because I remember her backing away from me, and then falling, and the knife was still in her.'

'Did she say anything to you?'

'No. She just had this . . . this terrible look on her face. Shocked and . . . and hurt . . . and . . . and like, wondering why I did it.'

'Where was the knife when she fell?'

'I don't know what you mean.'

'Was the knife on the *right*-hand side of her body or the *left*?'

'I don't know.'

'Try to remember.'

'I don't know. That was when I heard the front door opening and all I could think of was getting out of there.'

'When you stabbed her, did she *twist* away from you?'

'No. She backed away.'

'She didn't twist away while you were still holding the knife?'

'No. She moved straight back. As if she couldn't believe what I done, and . . . and just wanted to get *away* from me, you know?'

'And then she fell?'

'Yes. She . . . her knees sort of gave way and she grabbed for her belly, and her hands sort of . . . it was terrible . . . they just . . . they were grabbing *air*, you know? And she fell.'

'In what position?'

'On her side.'

'*Which* side?'

'I could still see the knife, so it must've been the opposite side. The side opposite from where I stabbed her.'

'Facing her, how was she lying on the floor? Show me.'

'Well . . .' Corwin rose from the bunk and stood before Carella. 'Let's say the toilet bowl there is the window, her feet were toward me, and her head was toward the window. So if you're me . . .' Corwin got on the floor and stretched his legs toward Carella 'This is the position she was in.'

'All right, now show me which side she was lying on.'

Corwin rolled onto his right side. 'This side,' he said.

'Her right side.'

'Yes.'

'And you saw the knife sticking out of the *opposite* side, the left side.'

'Yes.'

'Exactly where you'd stabbed her.'

'I suppose so, yes.'

'Was the knife still in that position when you broke the window and left the apartment?'

'I don't know. I didn't look at the knife again. Nor at her neither. I just wanted to get out of there fast. There was somebody coming, you understand?'

'One last question, Ralph. Was she dead when you went through that window?'

'I don't know. She was bleeding and . . . she was very quiet. I . . . guess she was dead. I don't know. I guess so.'

'Hello, Miss Simonov?'

'Yes.'

'Detective Kling, 87th Squad. I've . . .'

'Who?'

'Kling. Detective Kling. You remember we talked in the hallway . . .'

'Oh, yes, how are you?'

'Fine, thanks. I've been trying to get you all afternoon. It finally occurred to me, big detective that I am, that you probably work, and wouldn't be home until after five.'

'I *do* work,' Nora said, 'but I work right here in the apartment. I'm a freelance artist. I really *should* get an answering service, I suppose. I was uptown visiting my mother. I'm sorry you had trouble getting me.'

'Well,' Kling said, 'I've got you now.'

'Just barely. I still haven't taken off my coat.'

'I'll wait.'

'Would you? This apartment's stifling hot. If you close all the windows, they send up steam you could grow orchids with. And if you leave them open the tiniest crack, you come home and it's like an arctic tundra. I'll just be a minute. God, it's suffocating in here.'

Kling waited. While he waited, he looked at his copper bracelet. If the bracelet actually began working, he would send one to his aunt in San Diego, who had been suffering from rheumatism for close to fifteen years. If it didn't work, he would sue Meyer.

'Hello, I'm back.'

'Hello,' Kling said.

'Boy, that's much better,' Nora said. 'I can't stand extremes, can you? It's bitter cold in the street, and the temperature in here *has* to be at least a hundred and four. Wow. What were you calling about, Mr Kling?'

'Well, as you probably know, we apprehended the man who committed the Fletcher murder . . .'

'Yes, I read about it.'

'And the district attorney's office is now preparing the case against him. They called us this morning to ask whether you'd be available to make a positive identification of Corwin as the man you saw in the basement of the building.'

'Why is that necessary?'

'I don't follow you, Miss Simonov.'

'The newspapers said you had a full confession. Why do you need . . .'

'Yes, of course, but the prosecuting attorney still has to present evidence.'

'Why?'

'Well ... suppose, for example, that *I* confessed to the same murder, and it turned out *my* fingerprints were not on the knife, *I* was not the man you saw in the basement, *I* was in fact in Schenectady on the night of the murder, do you see what I mean? Confession or not, the DA has to make a case.'

'I see.'

'So what I'm calling about is to find out if you'd be willing to identify the man.'

'Yes, of course I would.'

'How about tomorrow morning?'

'What time tomorrow morning? I usually sleep late.'

'Name it.'

'First tell me where it'll be.'

'Downtown. On Arbor Street. Around the corner from the Criminal Courts Building.'

'Where's that?'

'The Criminal Courts Building? On High Street.'

'Oh. That's *all* the way downtown.'

'Yes.'

'Would eleven o'clock be too late?'

'No, I'm sure that'll be fine.'

'All right then.'

'I'll meet you downstairs in the lobby. That's 33 Arbor Street. At five to eleven, okay?'

'Yes, okay.'

'Unless I call you back. I want to check with the ...'

'When would you be calling back? If you called.'

'In the next two or three minutes. I just want to contact the DA's office to make sure ...'

'Oh, okay then. Because I want to take a bath.'

'If you don't hear from me within the next – let's say, five minutes, okay? – I'll see you in the morning.'

'Good.'

'Thank you, Miss Simonov.'

''Bye,' she said, and hung up.

6

Corwin's attorney, cockroach or otherwise, realized that, if he did not grant the DA's office permission to run a lineup on his client, they would simply get a Supreme Court judge to order such a lineup, so he agreed to it at once. He stipulated only that it be a *fair* lineup and that he be permitted to attend it. Rollie Chabrier, who was handling the case for the people, readily granted both of his demands.

A fair lineup meant that Corwin and the other men in the lineup should be dressed in approximately the same style of clothing, and should be of the same general build, height, and color. It would not have been considered fair, for example, if the other men in the lineup were all Puerto Rican midgets wearing clown costumes since the witness would then automatically eliminate them and identify the remaining man whether or not he was truly the one she had seen rushing in and out of the basement on the night of the murder. Rollie Chabrier chose men from the DA's detective squad, all of whom were about the same size and general build as Corwin, asked them all to dress casually, and then trotted them into his office together with Corwin himself, who was wearing civilian clothing for the occasion of his visit from Calcutta.

In the presence of Bert Kling, Nora Simonov, and Corwin's attorney – a cockroach, indeed, whose name was

Harvey Johns – Rollie Chabrier said, 'Miss Simonov, would you please look at these seven men and tell me if one of them is the man you saw in the basement of 721 Silvermine Oval on the night of December the twelfth, at or about 10:45 P.M.?'

Nora looked, and then said, 'Yes.'

'You recognize one of these men?'

'I do.'

'Which one is the man you saw in the basement?'

'That one,' Nora said, and pointed unerringly to Ralph Corwin.

The detectives from the DA's squad handcuffed Corwin once again, and walked him up the corridor to the elevator, which whisked him down ten floors to the basement of the building, where he was led up a ramp to a waiting police van that transported him back to Calcutta. In Chabrier's office, Harvey Johns thanked him for the fairness of the lineup he had run, and then advised him that his client had told him he no longer desired his services as defense attorney and that probably a new attorney would be appointed to the case, but this did not mean it had not been a pleasure working with Chabrier anyhow. Chabrier thanked Johns, and Johns went back to his office in midtown Isola. Chabrier also thanked Nora for her cooperation, and Kling for his assistance in getting Miss Simonov downtown, and then he shook hands with Kling, and walked them to the elevator, and said goodbye, and scurried off just before the elevator doors closed, a round, pink-checked man with a pencil-line mustache, wearing brown shoes with a dark blue suit. Kling figured he had Presidential aspirations.

In the marble entrance lobby of the building, Kling said, 'Now that was simple, wasn't it?'

'Yes,' Nora answered. 'And yet, I feel . . . I don't know. Somewhat like an informer, I guess. I realize the man *killed*

Sarah Fletcher, but at the same time I hate to think my identification will help convict him.' She shrugged, and then smiled suddenly and apologetically. 'Anyway, I'm glad it's over.'

'I'm sorry it was painful,' Kling said. 'Can the Department make amends by taking you to lunch?'

'Would it be the Department or would it be you?'

'Me, actually,' Kling said. 'What do you say?'

She had, Kling noticed, a direct approach to most matters, asking questions as guilelessly as a child, expecting honest answers in return. Without breaking her stride now, she turned her head toward him, long brown hair falling free over one eye, and said, 'If it's just lunch, fine.'

'That's all,' Kling said, and he smiled, but he could not hide his disappointment. He realized, of course, that he was still smarting from Cindy Forrest's abrupt termination of their relationship, and a nice way for a man to prove he was still attractive to women was to sweep someone like Nora Simonov off her feet and into his arms before Cindy could even raise her eyebrows in astonishment. But Nora Simonov wasn't having any, thanks. 'If it's just lunch, fine,' she had said, making it clear that she wasn't looking for any more meaningful relationship. She had caught the tone of Kling's reply, however, he knew that; her face was a direct barometer of her emotions, pressure-sensitive to every nuance of feeling within. She nibbled at her lip now, and said, 'I'm sorry, I didn't mean to make it sound so . . . terminal. It's just that I *am* in love with someone, you see, and I didn't want to give the impression that I might be, well, available, or interested, or . . . my God, I'm only screwing it up worse!'

'No, you're doing fine,' Kling said.

'I normally detest people who wear their hearts on their sleeves. *God*, are they boring! Anyway, do we have to have lunch, I'm not even hungry yet. What time is it?'

'A little after twelve.'

'Couldn't we walk a little and just talk? If we did, I wouldn't feel I was compromising my *grand amour*,' she said, rolling her eyes, 'and you wouldn't feel you were wasting lunch on a completely unresponsive dud.'

'I would love to walk and talk a little,' Kling said.

They walked.

The city that Thursday nine days before Christmas was overcast with menacing clouds; the weather bureau had promised a heavy snowfall before midafternoon. Moreover, a sharp wind was blowing in off the river, swirling in cruel eddies through the narrow streets of the financial district that bordered the municipal and federal courts. Nora walked with her head ducked against the wind, her fine brown hair whipping about her head with each fierce gust. As a defense against the wind, which truly seemed determined to blow her off the sidewalk, she took Kling's arm as they walked, and on more than one occasion turned her face into his shoulder whenever the blasts became too violent. Kling began wishing she hadn't already warned him off. As she chattered on about the weather and about how much she liked the look of the city just before Christmas, he entertained wild fantasies of male superiority: bold, handsome, witty, intelligent, sensitive cop pierces armor of young, desirable girl, stealing her away from ineffectual idiot she adores . . .

'The people, too,' Nora said. 'Something happens to them just before Christmas, they get, I don't know, grander in spirit.'

Young girl, in turn, realizing she has been waiting all these years for handsome witty, etc., cop lavishes adoration she had previously wasted on mealy-mouthed moron . . .

'Even though I recognize it's been brutalized and commercialized, it reaches me, it really does. And that's surprising because I'm Jewish, you know. We never celebrated Christmas when I was a little girl.'

'How old are you?' Kling asked.

'Twenty-four. Are you Jewish?'

'No.'

'Kling,' Nora said, and shrugged. 'It could be Jewish.'

'Is your boyfriend Jewish?'

'No, he's not.'

'Are you engaged?'

'Not exactly. But we do plan to get married.'

'What does he do?'

'I'd rather not talk about him, if you don't mind,' Nora said.

They did not talk about him again that afternoon. They walked through streets aglow with lighted Christmas trees, passing shop windows hung with tinsel and wreaths. Street-corner Santa Clauses jingled their bells and solicited dona-tions; Salvation Army musicians blew their tubas and trombones, shook their tambourines, and likewise asked for funds; shoppers hurried from store to store clutching gift-wrapped packages while overhead the clouds grew thicker and more menacing.

Nora told him that she usually kept regular working hours in the studio she had set up in one room of her large, rent-controlled apartment. ('Except once a week, when I go up to Riverhead to visit my mother, which is where I was all day yesterday while you were trying to reach me'), and that she did many different kinds of freelance design, from book jackets to theatrical posters, from industrial brochures to line drawings for cookbooks, color illustrations for children's books, and what-have-you. ('I'm usually kept very busy. It isn't just the art work, you know, it's running around to see editors and producers and authors and all sorts of people. I'll be *damned* if I'll give twenty-five percent of my income to an art agent. That's what some of them are getting these days, don't you think there should be a law?') She had studied art at Cooper Union in New York City, and then had gone on for more training at the Rhode Island School of Design, and then had come here a year ago to work for an advertising firm named Thadlow, Brunner, Growling and Crowe ('His name really was Growling, Anthony Growling') where she had lasted for little more than six months, doing illustrations of cans and cigarette packages and other such rewarding subjects before she'd decided to quit and begin freelancing. ('So that's the story of my life.')

It was almost three o'clock.

Kling suspected he was already halfway in love with her, but it was time to get back to the squadroom. He took her uptown in a taxi, and just before she got out in front of her building on Silvermine Oval, on the offchance that her earlier protestations of undying love were in the nature of a ploy, he said, 'I enjoyed this, Nora. Can I see you again sometime?'

She looked at him with an oddly puzzled expression, as though she had tried her best to make it abundantly clear that she was otherwise involved and had, through some dire fault of her own, failed to communicate the idea to him. She smiled briefly and sadly, shook her head, and said, 'No, I don't think so.'

Then she got out of the taxi and was gone.

Among Sarah Fletcher's personal effects that were considered of interest to the police before they arrested Ralph Corwin was an address book found in the dead woman's handbag on the bedroom dresser. In the Thursday afternoon stillness of the squadroom, Carella examined the book while Meyer and Kling discussed the potency of the copper bracelet Kling wore on his wrist. The squadroom was unusually quiet; a person could actually hear himself think. The typewriters were silent, the telephones were not ringing, there were no prisoners in the detention cage yelling their heads off about police brutality or human rights, and all the windows were tightly closed, shutting out even the noises of the street below. In deference to the calm (and also because Carella seemed so hard at work with Sarah Fletcher's address book), Meyer and Kling spoke in what amounted to whispers.

'I can only tell you,' Meyer said, 'that the bracelet is supposed to work miracles. Now what else can I tell you?'

'You can tell me how come it hasn't worked any miracles on *me* so far?'

'When did you put it on?' Meyer said.

'I marked it on my calendar,' Kling said. They were sitting in the corner of the squadroom closest to the detention cage, Kling in a wooden chair behind his desk, Meyer perched on one end of the desk. The desk was against the wall, and the wall was covered with departmental flyers, memos on new rules and regulations, next year's Detectives' Duty Chart (listing Night Duty, Day Duty, and Open Days for each of the squad's six detective teams), a cartoon clipped from the police magazine every red-blooded cop subscribed to, several telephone numbers of complainants Kling hoped to get back to before his tour ended, a photograph of Cindy Forrest (which he'd meant to take down), and several less-flattering mug shots of wanted criminals. Kling's calendar was buried under the morass on the wall; he had to take down an announcement for the PBA's annual New Year's Eve party to get at it. 'Here,' he said. 'You gave me the bracelet on December first.'

'And today's what?' Meyer asked.

'Today's the sixteenth.'

'How do you know I gave it to you on the first?'

'That's what the MB stands for. Meyer's bracelet.'

'All right, so that's exactly two weeks. So what do you expect? I told you it'd begin working in two weeks.'

'You said ten days.'

'I said two weeks.'

'Anyway, it's *more* than two weeks.'

'Listen, Bert, the bracelet works miracles, it can cure anything from arthritis to . . .'

'Then why isn't it working on me?'

'What do you expect?' Meyer asked. 'Miracles?'

There was nothing terribly fascinating about the alphabetical listings in Sarah Fletcher's address book. She had possessed a good handwriting, and the names, addresses, and telephone numbers were all clearly written and easily read. Even when she'd crossed out a telephone number to write in a new listing, the deletion was made with a single sure stroke of her pen, the new number written directly beneath it. Carella leafed through the pages, finding that most of the listings were for obviously married couples, (Chuck and Nancy Benton, Harold and Marie Spander, George and Ina Grossman, and on and on), some were for girlfriends, some for local merchants and service people, one for Sarah's hairdresser, another for her dentist, several for doctors, and a few for restaurants in town and across the river. A thoroughly uninspiring address book – until Carella came to a page at the end of the book, with the printed word MEMORANDA at its top.

'All I know,' Kling said, 'is that my shoulder still hurts. I'm lucky I haven't been in any fierce pistol duels lately, because I'm sure I wouldn't be able to draw my gun.'

'When's the last time you were in a fierce pistol duel?' Meyer asked.

'I'm in fierce pistol duels all the time,' Kling said, and grinned.

Under the single word MEMORANDA there were five names, addresses, and telephone numbers written in Sarah's meticulous hand. All of the names were men's names. They had obviously been entered in the book at different times because some were written in pencil and others in ink. The parenthetical initials following each entry were all noted in felt marking pens of various colors:

Andrew Hart
1120 Hall Avenue
622-8400
        (PB&G) (TG)

Michael Thornton
371 South Lindner
881-9371
        (TS)

Lou Kantor
434 North 16 Street
FR 7-2346
        (TPC) (TG)

Sal Decotto
831 Grover Avenue
FR5-3287
        (F)   (TG)

Richard Ferrer
110 Henderson
693-6648
        (QR) (TG)

If there was one thing Carella loved, it was a code. He loved a code almost as much as he loved German measles.

Sighing, he opened the top drawer of his desk and pulled out the Isola directory. He was verifying the address for the first name on Sarah Fletcher's MEMORANDA list when Kling said, 'There are some guys who won't let a case go, even after it's been solved.'

'Who did you have in mind?' Meyer asked.

'Certain very conscientious guys,' Kling said.

Carella pretended neither of them was there. The telephone book address for Andrew Hart matched the one in Sarah's handwriting. He flipped to the back of the directory.

'I knew a very conscientious cop one time,' Meyer said, and winked.

'Tell me about him,' Kling said, and winked back.

'He was walking a beat out in Bethtown, oh, this must have been three or four winters ago,' Meyer said. 'It was a bitter cold day, not unlike today, but he was a very conscientious man, this cop, and he walked his beat faithfully and well, without once taking a coffee break, or even stopping in any of the local bars for a nip.'

'He sounds like a stalwart,' Kling said, grinning.

Carella had found an address for Michael Thornton, the second name on Sarah's list. It, too, was identical to the one in her book.

'Oh, he *was* a stalwart, no question,' Meyer said. 'And conscientious as the day was long. Did I mention it was a bitter cold day?'

'Yes, I believe you did,' Kling said.

'Nonetheless,' Meyer said, 'it was the habit of a very pretty and well-built Bethtown lady to take a swim every day of the year, rain or shine, snow, hail, or sleet. Did I mention she had very big boobs?'

'I believe you did.'

Carella kept turning pages in the directory, checking names and addresses.

'The lady's house was right on the beach, and it was her habit to bathe stark naked because this was a very isolated part of Bethtown, way over near the end of the island. This was before they put the new bridge in, you still had to take a ferry to get out there. It so happened, however, that the lady's house was *also* on the conscientious cop's beat. And on this particularly bitter day some three or four winters ago, the lady rushed out of her back door with her arms crossed just below her big bulging boobs, hugging herself because it was so cold, and the conscientious cop . . .'

'Yes, yes, what about him?' Kling said.

'The conscientious cop took one look at that lady hugging herself as she ran down toward the water, and he yelled, "Stop, police!" and when the lady stopped, and faced him, still clutching herself under those big boobs, she indignantly asked, "What have I done, officer? What crime have I committed?" And the conscientious cop said, "It ain't what you *done*, lady, it's what you were *about* to do. You think I'm going to stand by while you drown those two chubby pink-nosed puppies?"'

Kling burst out laughing. Meyer slapped the top of his desk and roared at his own joke. Carella said, 'Will you guys please shut up?'

He had verified all five addresses.

In the morning, he would get to work.

The letter was the sixth one April Carella had written to Santa Claus. In the kitchen of the Riverhead house, she read it silently over her mother's shoulder:

Dear Santa,
I hope your not getting too
anoyed with my letters.
I no you must be bizy
this time of year. But
I thought of something,
and wud like to make a
change from my last letter.
Please dont bring the
Craftmaster Sewing
Kit, but insted I wud like
the Castle Toys doll
Bonnie that wets.
My Broter Mark will
be writen to you
personally about his
new idea. So long
for now, and regards.

April Carella

'What do you think, Mom?' she said.

She was standing behind her mother's chair, and Teddy could not see her lips, and had no idea that she had spoken. Teddy was a deaf mute, a beautiful woman with midnight hair and dark luminous brown eyes that cherished words because to her they were visible and tangible; she saw them forming as they tumbled from fingers; she touched them in the dark on her husband's lips, and heard them more profoundly than she would have with normal 'hearing.' She was thoroughly absorbed by the inconsistencies in her daughter's letter, and did not look up as April came around the chair. Why someone should be able to spell a word like 'personally' while making a shambles of simple words like 'busy' or 'would' was beyond Teddy's comprehension. Perhaps she should visit April's teacher, mildly suggest to her that whereas the child possessed undeniable writing ability, wouldn't her style be more effective if her imaginative spelling were controlled somewhat? Some of the avant-garde quality might be lost, true . . .

April touched her arm.

Teddy looked up into her daughter's face. The two, in the light of the Tiffany lamp that overhung the old oak table in the large kitchen, were something less than mirror images, but the resemblance, even for mother and daughter, was uncanny nonetheless. More remarkable, however, was the identical intensity of their expressions. As April repeated her question, Teddy studied her lips, and then raised her hands and slowly spelled out her answer, while April's gaze never faltered. It occurred to Teddy, with some amusement, that a child who could not spell 'would' might have difficulty deciphering the letters and words that Teddy deftly and fluidly formed with her fingers, especially when the message she was communicating was 'Your spelling is bad.' But April watched, nodding as she caught letters, smiling as the letters combined to form a word, and then another word, and finally grasping the short sentence, and saying, 'Which ones are spelled wrong, Mom? Show me?'

They were going over the letter again when April heard a key in the front door. Her eyes met briefly with her mother's. A smile cracked instantly across her face. Together, they rose instantly from the table. Mark, April's twin brother, was already bounding down the steps from his bedroom upstairs.

Carella was home.

7

At a little past eight the next morning, on the assumption that most men worked for a living and would be in transit to their jobs after that hour, Carella called Andrew Hart at the number listed in Sarah's address book. The phone was picked up on the fifth ring.

'Hello?' a man's voice said.

'Mr Hart?'

'Speaking.'

'This is Detective Carella of the 87th Squad. I wonder . . .'

'What's the matter?' Hart said immediately.

'I'd like to ask you some questions, Mr Hart.'

'I'm in the middle of shaving,' Hart said. 'I've got to leave for the office in a little while. What's this about?'

'We're investigating a homicide, Mr Hart . . .'

'A *what*? A homicide?'

'Yes, sir.'

'Who? Who's been killed?'

'A woman named Sarah Fletcher.'

'I don't know anyone named Sarah Fletcher,' Hart said.

'She seems to have known you, Mr Hart.'

'Sarah *who*? Fletcher, did you say?'

'That's right.'

'I don't know anybody by that name. Who says she knew me? I never heard of her in my life.'

'Your name's in her address book.'

'My what? My name? That's impossible.'

'Mr Hart, I have her book right here in my hand, and your name is in it, together with your address and your phone number.'

'Well, I don't know how it got there.'

'Neither do I. That's why I'd like to talk to you.'

'Okay, okay,' Hart said. 'What time is it? Jesus, is it ten after eight already?'

'Yes, it is.'

'Look, I've got to shave and get out of here. Can you come to the office later? About . . . ten o'clock? I should be free around then. I'd see you earlier, but someone's coming in at nine.'

'We'll be there at ten. Where is the office, Mr Hart?'

'On Hamilton and Reed. 480 Reed. The sixth floor. Hart and Widderman. We've got the whole floor.'

'See you at ten, Mr Hart.'

'Right,' Hart said, and hung up.

Like a woman in her tenth month, the clouds over the city twisted and roiled in angry discomfort but refused to deliver the promised snow. The citizens grew anxious. Hurrying to their jobs, dashing into subway kiosks, boarding buses, climbing into taxicabs, they glanced apprehensively at the bloated skies and wondered if the weather bureau, as usual, was wrong. To the average city dweller, being alerted to a snowstorm was like being alerted to the bubonic plague. Nobody in his right mind liked snow. Nobody liked putting on rubbers and galoshes and skid-chains and boots; nobody liked shoveling sidewalks and canceling dinner dates and missing theater parties; nobody liked slipping and sliding and falling on his ass. But worse than that, nobody liked being *promised* all that, and being forced to *anticipate* all that, and then not *having* all that delivered. The city dweller, for all his sophistication, was a creature of habit who dreaded any break in his normal routine. He would accept blackouts or garbage strikes or muggings in the park because these were not breaks in the routine, they *were* the routine. And besides, they reinforced the image he carried of himself as an urban twentieth-century swashbuckler capable of coping with the worst disasters. But threaten a taxicab strike and then postpone or cancel it? Promise a protest and have it dispersed by the police? Forecast snow and then have the storm hover indefinitely over the city like a writhing gray snake ready to strike? Oh no, you couldn't fool with a city person that way. It made him edgy and uncomfortable and insecure and constipated.

'So where the hell is it?' Meyer asked impatiently. One hand on the door of the police sedan, he looked up at the threatening sky and all but shook his fist at the gray clouds overhead.

'It'll come,' Carella said.

'When?' Meyer asked flatly, and opened the door, and climbed into the car. Carella started the engine. 'Damn forecasters *never* know what they're doing,' Meyer said. 'Last big storm we had, they were predicting sunny and mild. We can put men on the moon, but we can't tell if it's going to drizzle on Tuesday.'

'That's an interesting thing,' Carella said.

'What is?'

'About the moon.'

'What about the moon?'

'Why should everything down here be expected to work perfectly just because we've put men on the moon?'

'What the hell are you talking about?' Meyer said.

'We can put men on the moon,' Carella said, 'but we can't

get a phone call through to Riverhead. We can put men on the moon, but we can't settle a transit strike. We can put men on the moon . . .'

'I get your point,' Meyer said, 'but I fail to see the parallel. There is a connection between the weather and the billions of dollars we've spent shooting meteorological hardware into space.'

'I merely thought it was an interesting observation,' Carella said.

'It was very interesting,' Meyer said.

'What's the matter with *you* this morning?'

'Nothing's the matter with me this morning.'

'Okay,' Carella said, and shrugged.

They drove in silence. The city was a monochromatic gray, the backdrop for a Warner Brothers gangster film of the thirties. The color seemed to have been drained from everything – the most vivid billboards, the most vibrant building façades, the most lurid women's clothing, even the Christmas ornaments that decorated the shop windows. Overhung with eternal grayness, the trappings of the yuletide season stood revealed as shabby crap, tinsel and plastic to be exhibited once a year before being returned to the basement. In this bleak light, even the costumes of the streetcorner Santa Clauses appeared to be a faded maroon rather than a cheerful red, the fake beards dirty, the brass bells tarnished. The city had been robbed of sunshine and denied the cleansing release of snow. It waited, and it fretted, and it grew crankier by the minute.

'I was wondering about Christmas,' Carella said.

'What about it?'

'I've got the duty. You feel like switching with me?'

'What for?' Meyer said.

'I thought I'd give you Chanukah or something.'

'How long do you know me?' Meyer asked.

'Too long,' Carella said, and smiled.

'How many years has it been?' Meyer said. 'And you don't know I celebrate both Chanukah *and* Christmas? I've had a Christmas tree in the house ever since the kids were born. Every year. You've *been* there every year. You were there *last* year with Teddy. You *saw* the tree. Right in the living room. Right in the *middle* of the goddamn living room.'

'I forgot,' Carella said.

'I celebrate both,' Meyer said.

'Okay,' Carella said.

'Okay. So the answer is no, I don't want to switch the duty.'

'Okay.'

'Okay.'

In this mood of joyous camaraderie, Meyer and Carella parked the car and went into the building at 480 Reed Street, and up the elevator to the sixth floor – in silence. Hart and Widderman manufactured watchbands. A huge advertising display near the receptionist's desk in the lobby proudly proclaimed H&W BEATS THE BAND! and then backed the slogan with more discreet copy that explained how Hart and Widderman had solved the difficult engineering problems of the expansion watch bracelet to present to the world their amazing new line, all illustrated with photographs as big as Carella's head, in gleaming golden tones he felt certain he could hock at the nearest pawnshop. The receptionist's hair was almost as golden, but it did not look as genuine as that in the display. She glanced up from her magazine without much interest as the detectives approached her desk. Meyer was still reading the advertising copy, fascinated.

'Mr Hart, please,' Carella said.

'Who's calling?' the receptionist asked. She had a definite Calm's Point accent, and she sounded as if she were chewing gum, even though she was not.

'Detectives Carella and Meyer.'

'Just a minute, please,' she said, and lifted her phone, and pushed a button in the base. 'Mr Hart,' she said, 'there are some cops here to see you.' She listened for a moment, and then said, 'Yes, sir.' She replaced the receiver on its cradle, gestured toward the inside corridor with a nod of her golden tresses, said, 'Go right in, please. Door at the end of the hall,' and then went back to discovering what people were talking about in *Vogue*.

The gray skies had apparently got to Andrew Hart, too.

'You didn't have to broadcast to the world that the police department is here,' he said immediately.

'We merely announced ourselves,' Carella said.

'Well, okay, now you're here,' Hart said, 'let's get it over with.' He was a big man in his middle fifties, with iron-gray hair and black-rimmed eyeglasses. His eyes behind their lenses were brown and swift and cruel. His jacket was draped over the back of the chair behind his desk, and his shirt sleeves were rolled up over powerful forearms dense with black hair. A gold expansion bracelet, undoubtedly one of his own, held his watch fastened to his thick wrist. 'If you want to know the truth,' he said, 'I don't know what the hell you're doing here, anyway. I told you I don't know any Sarah Fletcher, and I don't.'

'Here's her book, Mr Hart,' Carella said, figuring there was no sense wasting time with a lot of bullshit. He handed the address book to Hart, opened to the MEMORANDA page. 'That's your name, isn't it?'

'Yeah,' Hart said, and shook his head. 'But how it got there is beyond me.'

'You don't know anybody named Sarah Fletcher, huh?'

'No.'

'Is it possible she's someone you met at a party, someone you exchanged numbers with . . .'

'No.'

'Are you married, Mr Hart?'

'What's that got to do with it?'

'*Are* you?'

'No.'

'We've got a picture of Mrs Fletcher, I wonder . . .'

'Don't go showing me any pictures of a corpse,' Hart said.

'This was taken when she was alive. It's a recent picture, it was on the dresser in her bedroom. Would you mind looking at it?'

'I don't see any sense in this at *all*,' Hart said. 'I told you I don't know her. How's looking at her picture . . . ?'

'Meyer?' Carella said, and Meyer handed him a manila envelope. Carella opened the flap and removed from the envelope a framed picture of Sarah Fletcher, which he handed to Hart. Hart looked at the photograph, and then immediately looked up at Carella.

'What is this?' he said.

'Do you recognize that picture, Mr Hart?'

'Let me see your badge,' Hart said.

'What?'

'Your badge, your badge. Let me see your identification.'

Carella took out his wallet, and opened it to where his detective's shield was pinned opposite his ID card. Hart studied both, and then said, 'I thought this might be a shakedown.'

'Why'd you think that?'

Hart did not answer. He looked at the photograph again, shook his head, and said, 'Somebody killed her, huh?'

'Yes, somebody did,' Carella answered. 'Did you know her?'

'I knew her.'

'I thought you said you didn't.'

'I didn't know Sarah Fletcher, if *that's* who you think she was. But I knew *this* broad, all right.'

'Who'd *you* think she was?' Meyer asked.

'Just who she told me she was.'

'Which was?'

'Sadie Collins. She introduced herself as Sadie Collins, and that's who I knew her as. Sadie Collins.'

'Where was this, Mr Hart? Where'd you meet her?'

'In a bar.'

'Where?'

'Who the hell remembers? A singles' bar. The city's full of them.'

'Would you remember when?'

'At least a year ago.'

'Ever go out with her?'

'Yes.'

'How often?'

'Often enough.'

'*How* often?'

'I used to see her once or twice a week.'

'*Used* to? When did you stop seeing her?'

'Last summer.'

'But until then you used to see her quite regularly.'

'Yeah, on and off.'

'Twice a week, you said.'

'Well, yeah.'

'Did you know she was married?'

'Who? Sadie? You're kidding.'

'She never told you she was married?'

'Never.'

'You saw her twice a week . . .'

'Yeah.'

'But you didn't know she was married?'

'How was I supposed to know that? She never said a word about it. Listen, there are enough single girls in this city, I don't have to go looking for trouble with somebody who's married.'

'Where'd you pick her up?' Meyer asked suddenly.

'I told you. A bar. I don't remember which . . .'

'When you went out, I mean.'

'What?'

'When you were going out, where'd you pick her up? At her apartment?'

'No. She used to come to my place.'

'Where'd you call her? When you wanted to reach her?'

'I didn't. She used to call me.'

'Where'd you go, Mr Hart? When you went out?'

'We didn't go out too much.'

'What *did* you do?'

'She used to come to my place. We'd spend a lot of time there.'

'But when you *did* go out . . .'

'Well, the truth is we never went out.'

'Never?'

'Never. She didn't want to go out much.'

'Didn't you think that was strange?'

'No.' Hart shrugged. 'I figured she liked to stay home.'

'If you never went out, what *did* you do, exactly, Mr Hart?'

'Well now, what the hell do you *think* we did, exactly?' Hart said.

'You tell us.'

'You're big boys. Figure it out for yourself.'

'Why'd you stop seeing her, Mr Hart?'

'I met somebody else. A nice girl. I'm very serious about her. That's why I thought . . .'

'Yes?'

'Nothing.'

'That's why you thought *what*, Mr Hart?'

'Okay, that's why I thought this was a shakedown. I thought somebody had found out about Sadie and me and . . . well . . . I'm very serious about this girl, I wouldn't want her to know anything about the past. About Sadie and me. About seeing Sadie.'

'What was so terrible about seeing Sadie?' Meyer asked.

'Nothing.'

'Then why would anyone want to shake you down?'

'I don't know.'

'If there was nothing terrible . . .'

'There wasn't.'

'Then what's there to hide?'

'There's nothing to hide. I'm just very serious about this girl, and I wouldn't want her to know . . .'

'To know what?'

'About Sadie.'

'Why not?'

'Because I just wouldn't.'

'Was there something wrong with Sadie?'

'No, no, she was a beautiful woman, beautiful.'

'Then why would you be ashamed . . . ?'

'Ashamed? Who said anything about being ashamed?'

'You said you wouldn't want your girlfriend . . .'

'Listen, what *is* this? I stopped seeing Sadie six months ago, I wouldn't even talk to her on the *phone* after that. If the crazy bitch got herself killed . . .'

'Crazy?'

Hart suddenly wiped his hand over his face, wet his lips, and walked behind his desk. 'I don't think I have anything more to say to you, gentlemen. If you have any other questions, maybe you'd better charge me with something, and I'll ask my lawyer's advice on what to do next.'

'What did you mean when you said she was crazy?' Carella asked.

'Good day, gentlemen,' Hart said.

In the lieutenant's corner office, Byrnes and Carella sat drinking coffee. Byrnes was frowning. Carella was waiting. Neither of the men said a word. A telephone rang in the squadroom outside, and Byrnes looked at his watch.

'Well, yes or no, Pete?' Carella asked at last.

'I'm inclined to say no.'

'Why?'

'Because I don't know why you still want to pursue this thing.'

'Oh come on, Pete! If the goddamn guy *did* it . . .'

'That's only *your* allegation. Suppose he *didn't* do it, and suppose *you* do something to screw up the DA's case?'

'Like what?'

'I don't know like what. They've got a grand jury indictment, they're preparing a case against Corwin, how the hell do I know what you might do? The way things are going these days, if you spit on the sidewalk that's enough to get a case thrown out of court.'

'Fletcher hated his wife,' Carella said calmly.

'Lots of men hate their wives. Half the men in this *city* hate their wives.'

'According to Hart . . .'

'All right, so she was playing around a little, so what? She had herself a little fling, who doesn't? Half the women in this *city* are having little flings right this minute.'

'*Her* little fling gives Fletcher a good reason for . . . look, Pete, what the hell *else* do we need? He had a motive, he had the opportunity, a golden one, in fact, and he had the means – another man's knife sticking out of Sarah's gut. What more do you want?'

'Proof. There's a funny little system we've got here in this city, Steve. It requires proof before we can arrest a man and charge him with murder.'

'Right. And all I'm asking is the opportunity to *try* for it.'

'Sure. By putting a tail on Fletcher. Suppose he sues the goddamn city?'

'For what?'

'He'll *think* of something.'

'Yes or no, Pete? I want permission to conduct a round-the-clock surveillance of Gerald Fletcher, starting Sunday morning. Yes or no?'

'I must be out of my mind,' Byrnes said, and sighed.

8

At 7:30 P.M. on the loneliest night of the week, Bert Kling did a foolish thing. He telephoned Nora Simonov. He did not expect her to be home, so he really did not know why he was calling her. He could only suppose that he was experiencing that great American illness known as the Saturday Night Funk, not to be confused with the Sunday Evening Hiatus or the Monday Morning Blues, none of which are daily newspapers.

The Saturday Night Funk (or the Snf, as it is familiarly known to those who have ever suffered from it) generally begins the night before, along about eight o'clock, when one realizes he does not have a date for that fabulous flight of **FUN** and **FRIVOLITY** known as S*A*T*U*R*D*A*Y N*I*G*H*T U*S*A.

There is no need for panic at this early juncture, of course. The mythical magical merriment is not scheduled to begin for at least another twenty-four hours, time yet to call a dozen birds or even a hundred, no need for any reaction more potent than a mild sort of self-chastisement for having been so tardy in making arrangements for the gay gaudy gala to follow. And should one fail to make a connection that Friday, there is still all day tomorrow to twirl those little holes in the telephone dial and ring up this or that hot number – Hello, sweetie, I was wondering whether you'd be available for an entertaining evening of enjoyment and eventual enervation – plenty of time, no need to worry.

By Saturday afternoon at about three, the first signs of anxiety begin to set in as this or that luscious lovely announces that, Oh my, I would have been thrilled and delighted to accompany you even into the mouth of a cannon, but oh goodness here it is Saturday afternoon already and you can't expect to call a girl at the last minute and have her free on D*A*T*E N*I*G*H*T U*S*A, can you? Last minute? What last minute? It is still only three in the afternoon, four in the afternoon, five in the evening. Evening? When did it become evening? And desperation pounces.

A quick brush of the hair, a sprinkle of cologne in the armpits, a bold adventurous approach to the phone (cigarette dangling from the lip), a nonchalant scanning of the little black book, a forthright dialing, and, Oh my, I would have adored going with you to the moon or even Jupiter and back, but here it is almost six o'clock on the most R*O*M*A*N*T*I*C N*I*G*H*T of the week, you don't expect a girl to be free at this late hour, do you? The Snf has arrived. It has arrived full-blown because it is now six o'clock, fast approaching seven, and at the stroke of seven-thirty you will turn into Spiro Agnew.

At the stroke of seven-thirty, Bert Kling called Nora Simonov, certain that she'd be out having a good time, like everybody else in the United States of America on this Saturday night.

'Hullo?' she said.

'Nora?' he said, surprised.

'Yes?'

'Hi. This is Bert Kling.'

'Hullo,' she said, 'what time is it?'

'Seven-thirty.'

'I must've fallen asleep. I was watching the six o'clock news.' She yawned and then quickly said, 'Excuse me.'

'Shall I call you back?'

'What for?'

'Give you a chance to wake up.'

'I'm awake, that's okay.'

The line went silent.

'Well . . . uh . . . how are you?' Kling asked.

'Fine,' Nora said, and the line went silent again.

In the next thirty seconds, as static crackled along the line and Kling debated asking the risky question that might prolong his misery eternally, he could not help realizing how spoiled he had been by Cindy Forrest, who, until four weeks ago at least, had been available at any hour of the day or night, and *especially* on Saturday, when no red-blooded American male should be left alone to weep into his wine.

'Well, I'm glad you're okay,' Kling said at last.

'Is that why you called? I thought maybe you had another suspect for me to identify,' Nora said, and laughed.

'No, no,' Kling said. 'No.' He laughed with her, immediately sobered, and quickly said, 'As a matter of fact, Nora, I was wondering . . .'

'Yes?'

'Would you like to go out?'

'What do you mean?'

'Out.'

'With you?'

'Yes.'

'Oh.'

In the next ten seconds of silence, which seemed much longer to Kling than the earlier thirty seconds of silence had been, he realized he had made a terrible mistake; he was staring directly into the double-barreled shotgun of rejection and about to have his damn fool head blown off.

'I told you, you know,' Nora said, 'that I'm involved with someone . . .'

'Yes, I know. Well, listen . . .'

'But I'm *not* doing anything tonight, and . . . if you want to go for a walk or something . . .'

'I thought maybe dinner.'

'Well . . .'

'And maybe dancing later.'

'Well . . .'

'I hate to eat alone, don't you?'

'Yes, as a matter of fact, I do. But Bert . . .'

'Yes?'

'I feel sort of funny about this.'

'Funny how?'

'Leading you on,' Nora said.

'I've been warned,' he said. 'You've given me fair warning.'

'I *would* like to have dinner with you,' Nora said, 'but . . .'

'Can you be ready at eight?'

'You do understand, don't you, that . . . ?'

'I understand completely.'

'Mmm,' she said dubiously.

'Eight o'clock?'

'Eight-thirty,' she said.

'See you then,' he said, and hung up quickly before she could change her mind. He was grinning when he looked into the mirror. He felt handsome and assured and sophisticated and in complete control of America.

He did not know who Nora's phantom lover was, but he was certain now that she was only playing the age-old maidenly game of shy resistance and that she would succumb soon enough to his masculine charm.

He was dead wrong.

*

Dinner was all right, he couldn't knock dinner. They exchanged thoughts on a wide variety of subjects:

'I once did a cover for a historical novel,' Nora said, 'with a woman wearing one of these very low-cut velvet gowns, you know, and I was bored to tears while I was doing the roughs, so I gave her three breasts. The art director didn't even notice. I painted out the third one when I did the final painting.'

'I look at myself,' Kling said, 'and I know I'm *not* a pig, I'm a fairly decent human being trying to do his job. And sometimes my job involves getting into situations that are distasteful to me. You think I *like* going onto a college campus and breaking up a protest by kids who don't want to die in a stupid war? But I'm also supposed to see that they don't burn down the administration building. So how do I convince them that keeping law and order, which is my job, is *not* the same as suppression? It gets difficult sometimes.'

'Contact sports,' Nora said, 'are all homosexual in nature, I'm convinced of it. You can't tell me the quarterback isn't copping a feel off the center every time he grabs that ball.'

And like that.

But after dinner, when Kling suggested that they go dancing at a little place he knew in the Quarter, three-piece band and nice atmosphere, Nora at first demurred, saying she was awfully tired and had promised her mother she would take her out to the cemetery early tomorrow morning, and then finally acquiescing when Kling said it was still only ten-thirty, and promised to have her home by midnight.

Pedro's, as Kling had promised, was long on atmosphere and good music. Dimly illuminated, ideal for lovers both married and un-, adulterated or pure, it seemed to work as a deterrent on Nora from the moment she stepped into the place. She was not good at hiding whatever she was feeling (as Kling had earlier noticed), and the ambience of Pedro's was either threatening or nostalgic (and possibly more), with the result that her eyes took on a glazed look, her mouth wilted, her shoulders slumped, she became the kind of Saturday-night date red-blooded American males feared and avoided; she became a thorough and complete pain in the ass.

Kling asked her to dance in the hope that bodily contact, blood pulsing beneath flesh, hands touching, cheeks brushing, all that jazz might speed along the seduction he had so successfully launched during dinner. But she held him at bay, with a rigid right arm on his left shoulder, so that eventually he tired physically of trying to draw her close, being afflicted with bursitis, and tired mentally of all the adolescent fumbling and maneuvering. He decided to ply her with booze, having been raised in a generation that placed strong store in the seductive powers of alcohol. (He was, incidentally, a cop who had tried pot twice and enjoyed it. He had realized, however, that he could not very well go around offering grass to young ladies, or even lighting up himself, and had abandoned that pleasant pastime.) Nora drank one drink, count it, or to be more exact, *half* a drink, toying with the remainder of it while Kling consumed two more and asked politely, 'Sure you don't want to drink up and have another?' To which she politely shook her head with a wan little smile.

And then, despite her protestations, two days ago, that she did not want to talk about her *grand amour*, the band began playing the Beatles' 'Something' and her eyes misted over, and the next thing Kling knew he was being treated to a monologue about her lover. The man, she confessed, had until just recently been married, and there were still some complications, but she expected they would be cleared up within the next several months, at which time she hoped to become his wife. She did not say what the complications were, but Kling surmised she was talking about a divorce settlement or some such; at this point, he could not have cared less. He had been warned, true, but spending a Saturday night with someone who talked about another man was akin to taking one's mother to a strip joint, maybe worse. He tried to change the subject, but the power of 'Something' prevailed, and, as the band launched into a second chorus, Nora similarly launched into *her* second chorus, so that the music seemed to be accompanying her little tone poem.

'We met entirely by accident,' she said, 'though we learned later that actually we could have met at any time during the past year.'

'Well, *most* people meet entirely by chance,' Kling said.

'Yes, of course, but this was just the most remarkable coincidence.'

'Mmm,' Kling said, and then launched into what he considered a provocative and perhaps completely original observation on The Beatles Phenomenon, remarking that their rise and fall had encompassed a mere five years or so, which seemed significant when one remembered that they were a product of the space age, where speed was of the essence and . . .

'He's so far superior to me,' Nora said, 'that sometimes I wonder what he sees in me at all.'

'What does he do for a living?' Kling asked, thinking Ho-hum.

Nora hesitated for only an instant. But because her face was such a meticulous recorder of anything she felt, he knew that what she said next would be a lie. He was suddenly terribly interested.

'He's a doctor,' Nora said, and turned her eyes from his, and lifted her drink, and sipped at it, and then glanced toward the bandstand.

'Is he on staff any place?'

'Yes,' she said immediately, and again, he knew she was lying. 'Isola General.'

'Over on Wilson Avenue?' he asked.

'Yes,' she said.

Kling nodded. Isola General was on Parsons and Lowell, bordering the River Dix.

'When do you expect to be married?' he asked.

'We haven't set the date yet.'

'What's his name?' Kling asked conversationally, and turned away from her, and lifted his own glass, and pretended to be completely absorbed in the band, which was now playing a medley of tunes from the forties, presumably for the Serutan members of their audience.

'Why do you want to know?' Nora asked.

'Just curious. I have a thing about names. I think certain names go together. If, for example, a woman named Freida did not eventually hook up with a man named Albert, I would be enormously surprised.'

'Who do you think a "Nora" should hook up with?'

'A "Bert?"' he said immediately and automatically, and was immediately sorry.

'She's *already* hooked up with someone whose name isn't "Bert."'

'What is his name?' Kling asked.

Nora shook her head. 'No,' she said. 'I don't think I'll tell you.'

It was twenty minutes to twelve.

True to his promise, Kling paid the check, hailed a taxicab, and took Nora home. She insisted that it wasn't necessary for him to come up in the elevator with her, but he told her there'd been a woman killed here in this very building less than a week ago, and since he was a cop and all, armed to the teeth and all, he might just as well accompany her. Outside the door to her apartment, she shook hands with him and said, 'Thank you, I had a very nice time.'

'Yes, me, too,' he answered, and nodded bleakly.

He got back to his apartment at 12:25, and the telephone rang some twenty minutes later. It was Steve Carella.

'Bert,' he said, 'I've arranged with Pete to put a twenty-four-hour tail on Fletcher, and I want to handle the first round myself. You think you can go with Meyer tomorrow when he hits Thornton?'

'Hits *who*?'

'The second guy in Sarah Fletcher's book.'

'Oh, sure, sure. What time's he going?'

'He'll be in touch with you.'

'Where are you, Steve? Home?'

'No, I've got the graveyard shift. Incidentally, there was a call for you.'

'Oh? Who called?'

'Cindy Forrest.'

Kling caught his breath. 'What'd she say?'

'Just to tell you she'd called.'

'Thanks,' Kling said.

'Good night,' Carella said, and hung up.

Kling put the receiver back on its cradle, took off his jacket, loosened his tie, and began unlacing his shoes. Twice he lifted the receiver from its cradle, began dialing Cindy's number, and changed his mind. Instead, he turned on the television in time to catch the one o'clock news. The weather forecaster announced that the promised snowstorm had blown out to sea. Kling got undressed, and went to bed.

9

Michael Thornton lived in an apartment building several blocks from the Quarter, close enough to absorb some of its artistic flavor, distant enough to escape its high rents. Kling and Meyer did not knock on Thornton's door until 11 A.M., on the theory that a man is entitled to sleep late on a Sunday morning, even if his name is listed in a dead lady's address book.

The man who opened the door was perhaps twenty-eight years old, with blond hair and a blond beard stubble. He was wearing pajama bottoms and socks, and his brown eyes were still edged with sleep. They had announced themselves as policemen through the wooden barrier of the closed door, and now the blond man looked at them bleary-eyed and asked to see their badges. He studied Meyer's shield, nodded, and, without moving from his position in the doorway, yawned and said, 'So what can I do for you?'

'We're looking for a man named Michael Thornton. Would you happen to be . . . ?'

'Mike isn't here right now.'

'Does he live here?'

'He lives here, but he isn't here right now.'

'Where is he?'

'What's this about?' the man said.

'Routine investigation,' Kling said.

The words 'routine investigation,' Kling noticed, never failed to strike terror into the hearts of man or beast. Had he said they were investigating a hatchet murder or a nursery school arson, the blond man's face would not have gone as pale, his eyes would not have begun to blink the way they did. In the land of supersell, the understatement – 'routine investigation' – was more powerful than trumpets and kettle-drums. The blond man was visibly frightened and thinking furiously. Somewhere in the building, a toilet flushed. Meyer and Kling waited patiently.

'Do you know where he is?' Kling said at last.

'Whatever this is, I know he had nothing to do with it.'

'It's just a routine investigation,' Kling repeated, and smiled.

'What's *your* name?' Meyer asked.

'Paul Wendling.'

'Do you live here?'

'Yes.'

'Do you know where we can find Michael Thornton?'

'He went over to the shop.'

'What shop?'

'We have a jewelry shop in the Quarter. We make silver jewelry.'

'The shop's open today?'

'Not to the public. We're not violating the law, if that's what you're thinking.'

'If you're not open to the public . . .'

'Mike's working on some new stuff. We make our jewelry in the back of the shop.'

'What's the address there?' Meyer asked.

'1156 Hadley Place.'

'Thank you,' Meyer said.

Behind them, Paul Wendling watched as they went down the steps, and then quickly closed the door.

'You know what he's doing right this minute?' Meyer asked.

'Sure,' Kling said. 'He's calling his pal at the shop to tell him we're on the way over.'

Michael Thornton, as they had guessed, was not surprised to see them. They held up their shields to the plate-glass entrance door, but he was clearly expecting them, and he unlocked the door at once.

'Mr Thornton?' Meyer asked.

'Yes?'

He was wearing a blue work smock, but the contours of the garment did nothing to hide his powerful build. Wide-shouldered, barrel-chested, thick forearms and wrists showing below the short sleeves of the smock, he backed away from the door like a boulder moving on ball bearings and allowed them to enter the shop. His eyes were blue, his hair black. A small scar showed white in the thick eyebrow over his left eye.

'We understand you're working,' Meyer said. 'Sorry to break in on you this way.'

'That's okay,' Thornton said. 'What's up?'

'You know a woman named Sarah Fletcher?'

'No,' Thornton said.

'You know a woman named Sadie Collins?'

Thornton hesitated. 'Yes,' he said.

'This the woman?' Meyer asked, and showed him a newly made stat of the photograph they had confiscated from the Fletcher bedroom.

'That's Sadie. What about her?'

They were standing near Thornton's showcase, a four-foot-long glass box on tubular steel legs. Rings, bracelets, necklaces, pendants dizzily reflected the sunshine that slanted through the front window of the shop. Meyer took his time putting the stat back into his notebook, meanwhile giving Kling a chance to observe Thornton. The picture seemed to have had no visible effect on him. Like the solid mass of mountain that he was, he waited silently, as though challenging the detectives to scale him.

'What was your relationship with her?' Kling said.

Thornton shrugged. 'Why?' he asked. 'Is she in trouble?'

'When's the last time you saw her?'

'You didn't answer my question,' Thornton said.

'Well, you didn't answer ours, either,' Meyer said, and smiled. 'What was your relationship with her, and when did you see her last?'

'I met her in July and the last time I saw her was in August. We had a brief hot thing, and then good-bye.'

'Where'd you meet her?'

'In a joint called The Saloon.'

'Where's that?'

'Right around the corner. Near what used to be the legit theater there. The one that's showing skin flicks now. The Saloon's a bar, but they also serve sandwiches and soup. It's not a bad joint. It gets a big crowd, especially on weekends.'

'Singles?'

'Mostly. A couple of fags thrown in for spice. But it's not a gay bar, not by the usual definition.'

'And you say you met Sadie in July?'

'Yeah. The beginning of July. I remember because I was supposed to go out to Greensward that weekend, but the broad who was renting the bungalow already invited ten other people to the beach, so I got stuck here in the city. You ever get stuck here in the city on a weekend in July?'

'Occasionally,' Meyer said dryly.

'How'd you happen to meet her?' Kling asked.

'She admired the ring I was wearing. It was a good opening gambit because the ring happened to be one of my own.' Thornton paused. 'I designed it and made it. Here at the shop.'

'Was she alone when you met her?' Kling asked.

'Alone and lonely,' Thornton said, and grinned. It was a knowing grin, a grin hoping for a similar grin in response from Kling and Meyer, who, being cops, had undoubtedly seen and heard all kinds of things and were therefore men of the world, as was Thornton himself, comrades three who knew all about lonely women in singles' bars.

'Did you realize she was married?' Kling asked, sort of spoiling the Three Musketeers image.

'No. Is she?'

'Yes,' Meyer said. Neither of the detectives had yet informed Thornton that the lady in question, Sarah or Sadie or both, was now unfortunately deceased. They were saving that for last, like dessert.

'So what happened?' Kling said.

'Gee, I didn't know she was married,' Thornton said, seeming truly surprised. 'Otherwise *nothing* would've happened.'

'What *did* happen?'

'I bought her a few drinks, and then I took her home with me. I was living alone at the time, the same pad on South Lindner, but alone. We balled, and then I put her in a cab.'

'When did you see her next?'

'The following day. It was goofy. She called me in the morning, said she was on her way downtown. I was still in bed. I said, "So come on down, baby." And she did. *Believe* me, she did.' Thornton grinned his man-of-the-world grin again, inviting Kling and Meyer into his exclusive all-male club that knew all about women calling early in the morning to say they were on their way down, baby. Somehow, Kling and Meyer did not grin back.

Instead, Kling said, 'Did you see her again after that?'

'Two or three times a week.'

'Where'd you go?'

'To the pad on South Lindner.'

'Never went any place but there?'

'Never. She'd give me a buzz on the phone, say she was on her way, and was I ready? Man, I was *always* ready for her.'

'Why'd you quit seeing her?'

'I went out of town for a while. When I got back, I just didn't hear from her again.'

'Why didn't you call her?'

'I didn't know where to reach her.'

'She never gave you her phone number?'

'Nope. Wasn't listed in the directory, either. No place in the city. I tried all five books.'

'Speaking of books,' Kling said, 'what do you make of this?'

He opened Sarah Fletcher's address book to the MEMO-RANDA page and extended it to Thornton. Thornton studied it and said, 'Yeah, what about it? She wrote this down the night we met.'

'You saw her writing it?'

'Sure.'

'Did she write those initials at the same time?'

'What initials?'

'The ones in parentheses. Under your phone number.'

Thornton studied the page more closely. 'How would I know?' he said, frowning.

'You said you saw her writing . . .'

'Yeah, but I didn't see the actual page, I mean, we were in *bed*, man, this was like after the second time around, and she asked me what the address was, and how she could get in touch with me, and I told her. But I didn't actually see the page itself. I only saw her writing in the book, you dig?'

'Got any idea what the initials mean?'

'TS can only mean "Tough Shit,"' Thornton said, and grinned.

'Any reason why she might want to write that in her book?' Meyer asked.

'Hey, I'm only kidding,' Thornton said, the grin expanding. 'We had a ball together. Otherwise, why'd she keep coming back for more?'

'Who knows? She *stopped* coming back, didn't she?'

'Only because I went out of town for a while.'

'How long a while?'

'Four days,' Thornton said. 'I went out to Arizona to pick up some Indian silver. We sell some crap here, too, in addition to what Paul and I make.'

'Gone only four days, and the lady never called again,' Kling said.

'Yeah, well, maybe she got sore. I left kind of sudden like.'

'What day was it?'

'Huh?'

'The day you left?'

'I don't know. Why? The middle of the week, I guess. I don't remember. Anyway, who cares?' Thornton said. 'There are plenty of broads in this city. What's one more or less?' He shrugged, and then looked suddenly thoughtful.

'Yes?' Meyer said.

'Nothing. Just . . .'

'Yes?'

'She was kind of special, I have to admit it. I mean, she wasn't the kind of broad you'd take home to mother, but she was something else. She was *really* something else.'

'How do you mean?'

'She was . . .' Thornton grinned. 'Let's put it this way,' he said. 'She took me places I'd never been before, you know what I mean?'

'No, what do you mean?' Kling said.

'Use your imagination,' Thornton said, still grinning.

'I can't,' Kling answered. 'There's no place I've never been before.'

'Sadie would've *found* some for you,' Thornton said, and the grin suddenly dropped from his face. 'She'll call again, I'm sure of it. She's got my number right there in her book, she'll call.'

'I wouldn't count on it,' Meyer said.

'Why not? She kept coming back, didn't she? We had . . .'

'She's dead,' Meyer said.

They kept watching his face. It did not crumble, it did not express grief, it did not even express shock. The only thing it expressed was sudden anger.

'The stupid twat,' Thornton said. 'That's all she ever was, a stupid twat.'

Police work (like life) is often not too tidy. Take surveillance, for example. On Friday afternoon, Carella had asked Byrnes for permission to begin surveillance of Gerald Fletcher on Sunday morning. Being a police officer himself, and knowing that police work (like life) is often not too tidy, Byrnes never once thought of asking Carella why he would not prefer to start his surveillance the very next day, Saturday, instead of waiting two days. The reason Carella did not choose to start the very next day was that police work (like life) is often not too tidy – as in the case of the noun 'surveillance' and the noun/adjective 'surveillant,' neither of which has a verb to go with it in the English language.

Carella had 640 odds-and-ends to clean up in the office on Saturday before he could begin the surveillance of Gerald Fletcher with anything resembling an easy conscience. So he had spent the day making phone calls and typing up reports and generally trying to put things in order. In all his years of police experience, he had never known a criminal who was so considerate of a policeman's lot that he would wait patiently for one crime to be solved before committing another. There were four burglaries, two assaults, a robbery, and a forgery still unsolved in Carella's case load; the least he could do was try to create some semblance of order from the information he had on each before embarking on a lengthy and tedious surveillance. Besides, surveillance (like police work) is often not too tidy.

On Sunday morning, Carella was ready to become a surveillant. That is to say, he was ready to adopt a surveillant stance and thereby begin surveillance of his suspect. The trouble was, just as the English language had been exceptionally untidy in not having stolen the verb from the French when it swiped the noun and the adjective, a surveillance (like life and like police work) is bound to get untidy if there is nobody to *surveille*.

Gerald Fletcher was nowhere in sight.

Carella had started his surveillance with the usual police gambit of calling Fletcher's apartment from a nearby phone booth early in the morning. The object of this sometimes transparent ploy was to ascertain that the suspect was still in his own digs, after which the police tail would wait downstairs for him to emerge and then follow him to and fro wherever he went. Gerald Fletcher, however, was *not* in his digs. This being Sunday morning, Carella automatically assumed that Fletcher was spending the weekend elsewhere. But, intrepid law enforcer he, and steadfast surveillant besides, he parked the squad's new (used) 1970 Buick sedan across the street from Fletcher's apartment building, and alternately watched the front door of 721 Silvermine Oval and the kids playing in the park, thinking that perhaps Fletcher had merely spent

S*A*T*U*R*D*A*Y N*I*G*H*T someplace and might return home momentarily.

At twelve noon, Carella got out of the car, walked into the park, and sat on a bench facing the building. He ate the ham and cheese sandwich his wife had prepared for him, and drank a soft drink that beat the others cold but wasn't so hot hot. Then he stretched his legs by walking over to the railing that overlooked the river, never taking his eyes off the building, and finally went back to the car. His vigil ended at 5 P.M., when he was relieved by Detective Arthur Brown, driving the squad's old 1968 Chevrolet sedan. Brown was equipped with a description of Fletcher as well as a photograph swiped from the bedroom dresser in Fletcher's apartment. In addition, he knew what sort of automobile Fletcher drove, courtesy of the Motor Vehicle Bureau. He told Carella to take it easy, and then he settled down to the serious business of watching a doorway for the next seven hours, at which time he was scheduled to be relieved by O'Brien, who would hold the fort until eight in the morning, when Kapek would report to work for the long daytime stretch.

Carella went home to read his son's latest note to Santa Claus, and then he had dinner with the family and was settling down in the living room with a novel he had bought a week ago and had not yet cracked, when the telephone rang.

'I've got it!' he yelled, knowing that Teddy could not hear him, and knowing this was Fanny's day off, but also knowing that Mark, his son, had a habit these days of answering the telephone with the words 'Automobile Squad, Carella here,' all well and good unless the *caller* happened to be a detective from the Automobile Squad trying to report on a stolen vehicle.

'Hello?' Carella said into the mouthpiece.

'Hello, Steve?'

'Yes?' Carella said. He did not recognize the voice.

'This is Gerry.'

'Who?'

'Gerry Fletcher.'

Carella almost dropped the receiver. 'Hello,' he said, 'how are you?'

'Fine, thanks. I was away for the weekend, just got back a little while ago, in fact. I frankly find this apartment depressing as hell. I was wondering if you'd like to join me for a drink.'

'Well,' Carella said, 'it's late, and I was just about to . . .'

'Nonsense, it's not even eight o'clock.'

'Yes, but it's Sunday night . . .'

'Hop in your car and meet me down here,' Fletcher said. 'We'll do a little old-fashioned pub crawling, what the hell.'

'No, I really couldn't. Thanks a lot, Gerry, but . . .'

'Take you half an hour to get here,' Fletcher said, 'and you may end up saving my life. If I sit here alone another five minutes, I'm liable to throw myself out the window.' He suddenly began laughing. 'You know what the Penal Law has to say about suicide, don't you?'

'No, what?' Carella asked.

'Silliest damn section in the book,' Fletcher said, still laughing. 'It says, and I quote "*Although suicide is deemed a grave public wrong, yet from the impossibility of reaching the successful perpetrator, no forfeiture is imposed.*" How do you like that for legal nonsense? Come on, Steve. I'll show you some of the city's brighter spots, we'll have a few drinks, what do you say?'

It suddenly occurred to Carella that Gerald Fletcher had *already* had a few drinks before placing his call. It further occurred to him that if he played this *too* cozily, Fletcher might rescind his generous offer. And since there was nothing Carella wanted more than a night on the town with a murder suspect who might possibly drink more than was prudent for his own best interests, he immediately said, 'Okay, I'll see you at eight-thirty. Provided I can square it with my wife.'

'Good,' Fletcher said. 'See you.'

10

Paddy's Bar & Grille was on the Stem, adjacent to the city's theater district. Carella and Fletcher got there at about nine o'clock, while the place was still relatively quiet. The action began a little later, Fletcher explained, the operative theory behind a singles operation being that neither bachelor nor career girl should seem too obvious about wanting to make each other's acquaintance. If you began to prowl too early, you appeared eager. If you got there too late, however, you missed out. The idea was to time your arrival just as the crowd was beginning to reach its peak, wandering in as though casually looking for a phone booth instead of a partner.

'You seem to know a lot about it,' Carella said.

'I'm an observant man,' Fletcher said, and smiled. 'What are you drinking?'

'Scotch and soda,' Carella said.

'A scotch and soda,' Fletcher said to the bartender, 'and a Beefeater's martini, straight up.'

He had drunk whiskey sours the day they'd had lunch together, Carella remembered, but he was drinking martinis tonight. Good. The more potent the drinks, the looser his tongue might become. Carella looked around the room. The men ranged in age from the low thirties to the late fifties, a scant dozen in the place at this early hour, all of them neatly dressed in city weekend clothes, sports jackets and slacks, some wearing shirts and ties, others wearing shirts with ascots, still others wearing turtlenecks. The women, half in number, were dressed casually as well – pants suits, skirts, blouses or sweaters, with only one brave and rather ugly soul dressed to the teeth in a silk Pucci. The mating game, at this hour, consisted of sly glances and discreet smiles; no one was willing to take a real gamble until he'd had an opportunity to look over the entire field.

'What do you think of it?' Fletcher asked.

'I've seen worse,' Carella said.

'I'll bet you have. Would it be fair to say you've also seen better?' Their drinks arrived at that moment, and Fletcher lifted his glass in a silent toast. 'What kind of person would you say comes to a place like this?' he asked.

'Judging from appearances alone, and it's still early . . .'

'It's a fairly representative crowd,' Fletcher said.

'I would say we've got a nice lower-middle-class clientele bent on making contact with members of the opposite sex.'

'A pretty decent element, would you say?'

'Oh, yes,' Carella answered. 'You go into some places, you know immediately that half the people surrounding you are thieves. I don't smell that here. Small businessmen, junior executives, divorced ladies, bachelor girls – for example, there isn't a hooker in the lot, which is unusual for a bar on the Stem.'

'Can you recognize a hooker by just looking at her?'

'Usually.'

'What would you say if I told you the blonde in the Pucci is a working prostitute?'

Carella looked at the woman again. 'I don't think I'd believe you.'

'Why not?'

'Well, to begin with, she's a bit old for the young competition parading the streets these days. Secondly, she's in deep conversation with a plump little girl who undoubtedly came down from Riverhead looking for a nice boy she can bed and eventually marry. And thirdly, she's not *selling* anything. She's waiting for one of those two or three older guys to make their move. Hookers don't wait, Gerry. *They* make the approach, *they* do the selling. Business is business, and time is money. They can't afford to sit around being coy.' Carella paused. '*Is* she a working prostitute?'

'I haven't the faintest idea,' Fletcher said. 'Never even saw her before tonight. I was merely trying to indicate that appearances can sometimes be misleading. Drink up, there are a few more places I'd like to show you.'

He knew Fletcher well enough, he thought, to realize that the man was trying to tell him something. At lunch last Tuesday, Fletcher had transmitted a message and a challenge: *I killed my wife, what can you do about it?* Tonight, in a similar manner, he was attempting to indicate something else, but Carella could not fathom exactly what.

Fanny's was only twenty blocks away from Paddy's Bar & Grille, but as far removed from it as the moon. Whereas the first bar seemed to cater to a quiet crowd peacefully pursuing its romantic inclinations, Fanny's was noisy and raucous, jammed to the rafters with men and women of all ages, wearing plastic hippie crap purchased in head shops up and down Jackson Avenue. If Paddy's had registered a seven on the scale of desirability and respectability, Fanny's rated a four. The language sounded like what Carella was used to hearing in the squadroom or in any of the cellblocks at Calcutta. There were half a dozen hookers lining the bar, suffering severely from the onslaught of half a hundred girls in skin-tight costumes wiggling their behinds and thrusting their breasts at anything warm and moving. The approaches were blatant and unashamed. There were more hands on asses than Carella could count, more meaningful glances and ardent sighs than seemed possible outside of a bedroom, more invitations than Truman Capote had sent out for his last masked ball. As Carella and Fletcher elbowed their way toward the bar, a brunette, wearing a short skirt and a see-through blouse without a bra, planted herself directly in Carella's path and said, 'What's the password, stranger?'

'Scotch and soda,' Carella said.

'Wrong,' the girl answered, and moved closer to him.

'What is it then?' he asked.

'Kiss me,' she said.

'Some other time,' he answered.

'That isn't a command,' she said, giggling, 'it's only the password.'

'Good,' he said.

'So if you want to get to the bar,' the girl said, 'say the password.'

'Kiss me,' he said, and was moving past her when she threw her arms around his neck and delivered a wet, open-mouthed, tongue-writhing kiss that shook him to his socks. She held the kiss for what seemed like an hour and a half, and then, with her arms still around his neck, she moved her head back a fraction of an inch, touched her nose to his, and said, 'I'll see you later, stranger. I have to go to the Ladies.'

At the bar, Carella wondered when he had last kissed anyone but his wife, Teddy. As he ordered a drink, he felt a soft pressure against his arm, turned to his left, and found one of the hookers, a black girl in her twenties, leaning in against him and smiling.

'What took you so long to get here?' she said. 'I've been waiting all night.'

'For what?' he said.

'For the good time I'm going to show you.'

'Wow, have *you* got the wrong number,' Carella said, and turned to Fletcher, who was already lifting his martini glass.

'Welcome to Fanny's,' Fletcher said, and raised his glass in a toast, and then drank the contents in one swallow and signaled to the bartender for another. 'You will find many of them on exhibit,' he said.

'Many what?'

'Many fannies. And other things as well.' The bartender brought a fresh martini with lightning speed and grace. Fletcher lifted the glass. 'I hope you don't mind if I drink myself into a stupor,' he said.

'Go right ahead,' Carella answered.

'Merely pour me into the car at the end of the night, and I'll be eternally grateful.' Fletcher lifted the glass and drank. 'I don't usually consume this much alcohol,' he said, 'but I'm very troubled about that boy . . .'

'What boy?' Carella said immediately.

'Listen, honey,' the black hooker said, 'aren't you going to buy a girl a drink?'

'Ralph Corwin,' Fletcher said. 'I understand he's having some difficulty with his lawyer, and . . .'

'Don't be such a tight-ass,' the girl said. 'I'm thirsty as hell here.'

Carella turned to look at her. Their eyes met and locked. The girl's look said, What do you say? Do you want it or not? Carella's look said, Honey, you're asking for big trouble. Neither of them exchanged a word. The girl got up and moved four stools down the bar, to sit next to a middle-aged man wearing bell-bottomed suede pants and a tangerine-colored shirt with billowing sleeves.

'You were saying?' Carella said, turning again to Fletcher.

'I was saying I'd like to help Corwin somehow.'

'*Help* him?'

'Yes. Do you think Rollie Chabrier would consider it strange if I suggested a good defense lawyer for the boy?'

'I think he might consider it passing strange, yes.'

'Do I detect a note of sarcasm in your voice?'

'Not at all. Why, I'd guess that ninety percent of all men whose wives have been murdered will then go out and recommend a good defense lawyer for the accused murderer. You've *got* to be kidding.'

'I'm not. Look, I know that what I'm about to say doesn't go over very big with you . . .'

'Then don't say it.'

'No, no, I *want* to say it.' Fletcher took another swallow of his drink. 'I feel sorry for that boy. I feel . . .'

'Hello, stranger.' The brunette was back. She had taken the stool vacated by the hooker, and now she looped her arm familiarly through Carella's and asked, 'Did you miss me?'

'Desperately,' he said. 'But I'm having a very important conversation with my friend here, and . . .'

'Never mind your friend,' the girl said. 'I'm Alice Ann, who are you?'

'I'm Dick Nixon,' Carella said.

'Nice to meet you, Dick,' the girl answered. 'Would you like to kiss me again?'

'No.'

'Why not?'

'Because I have these terrible sores inside my mouth,' Carella said, 'and I wouldn't want you to catch them.'

Alice Ann looked at him and blinked. She reached for his drink then, apparently wishing to wash her possibly already contaminated mouth, realized it was *his* filthy drink, turned immediately to the man on her left, pushed his arm aside, grabbed his glass, and hastily swallowed a mouthful of disinfectant alcohol. The man said, 'Hey!' and Alice Ann said, 'Cool it, Buster,' and got off the stool, throwing Carella a look even more scorching than her kiss had been, and swiveling off toward a galaxy of young men glittering in a corner of the crowded room.

'You won't understand this,' Fletcher said, 'but I feel grateful to that boy. I'm glad he killed her, and I'd hate to see him punished for what I consider an act of mercy.'

'Take my advice,' Carella said. '*Don't* suggest this to Rollie. I don't think he'd understand.'

'Do *you* understand?' Fletcher asked.

'Not entirely,' Carella said.

Fletcher finished his drink. 'Let's get the hell out of here,' he said. 'Unless you see something you want.'

'I already *have* everything I want,' Carella answered, and wondered if he should tell Teddy about the brunette in the peekaboo blouse.

The Purple Chairs was a bar farther downtown, apparently misnamed, since everything in the place was purple *except* the chairs. Ceiling, walls, bar, tables, curtains, napkins, mirrors, lights, all were purple. The chairs were white.

The misnomer was intentional.

The Purple Chairs was a Lesbian bar, and the subtle question being asked was: Is everybody out of step but Johnny? The chairs were white. Pure. Pristine. Innocent. Virginal. Then why insist on calling them purple? Where did perversity lie, in the actuality or in the labeling?

'Why here?' Carella asked immediately.

'Why not?' Fletcher answered. 'I'm showing you some of the city's more frequented spots.'

Carella strenuously doubted that this was one of the city's more frequented spots. It was now a little past eleven, and the place was only sparsely populated, entirely by women – women talking, women smiling, women dancing to the jukebox, women touching, women kissing. As Carella and

Fletcher moved toward the bar, tended by a bull dagger with shirt sleeves rolled up over her powerful forearms, a rush of concerted hostility focused upon them like the beam of a death ray. The bartender verbalized it.

'Sightseeing?' she asked.

'Just browsing,' Fletcher answered.

'Try the public library.'

'It's closed.'

'Maybe you're not getting my message.'

'What's your message?'

'Is anybody bothering *you*?' the bartender asked.

'No.'

'Then stop bothering *us*. We don't need you here, and we don't want you here. You like to see freaks, go to the circus.' The bartender turned away, moving swiftly to a woman at the end of the bar.

'I think we've been invited to leave,' Carella said.

'We certainly haven't been invited to stay,' Fletcher said. 'Did you get a good look?'

'I've been inside dyke bars before.'

'Really? My first time was in September. Just goes to show,' he said, and moved unsteadily toward the purple entrance door.

The cold December air worked furiously on the martinis Fletcher had consumed, so that by the time they got to a bar named Quigley's Rest, just off Skid Row, he was stumbling along drunkenly and clutching Carella's arm for support. Carella suggested that perhaps it was time to be heading home, but Fletcher said he wanted Carella to see them all, see them all, and then led him into the kind of joint Carella had mentioned earlier, where he knew instantly that he was stepping into a hangout frequented by denizens, and was instantly grateful for the .38 holstered at his hip. The floor of Quigley's Rest was covered with sawdust, the lights were dim, the place at twenty minutes to midnight was crowded with people who had undoubtedly awoken at 10 P.M. and who would go till ten the next morning. There was very little about their external appearances to distinguish them from the customers in the first bar Fletcher and Carella had visited. They were similarly dressed, they spoke in the same carefully modulated voices, they were neither as blatant as the crowd in Fanny's nor as subdued as the crowd in The Purple Chairs. But if a speeding shark in cloudy water can still be distinguished from a similarly speeding dolphin, so were the customers in Quigley's immediately identified as dangerous and deadly. Carella was not sure that Fletcher sensed this as strongly as he, himself, did. He knew only that he did not wish to stay here long, especially with Fletcher as drunk as he was.

The trouble started almost at once.

Fletcher shoved his way into position at the bar, and a thin-faced young man wearing a dark blue suit and a flowered tie more appropriate to April than December turned toward him sharply and said, 'Watch it.' He barely whispered the words, but they hung on the air with deadly menace, and before Fletcher could react or reply, the young man shoved the flat of his palm against Fletcher's upper arm, with such force that he knocked him to the floor. Fletcher blinked up at him, and started to get drunkenly to his feet. The young man suddenly kicked him in the chest, a flatfooted kick that was less powerful than the shove had been but had the same effect. Fletcher fell back to the floor again, and this time his head crashed heavily against the sawdust. The young man swung his body in preparation for another kick, this time aiming it at Fletcher's head.

'That's it,' Carella said.

The young man hesitated. Still poised on the ball of one foot, the other slightly back and cocked for release, he looked at Carella and said, '*What's* it?' He was smiling. He seemed to welcome the opportunity of taking on another victim. He turned fully toward Carella now, balancing his weight evenly on both feet, fists bunched. 'Did you say something?' he asked, still smiling.

'Pack your bag, sonny,' Carella said, and bent down to help Fletcher to his feet. He was prepared for what happened next, and was not surprised by it. The only one surprised was the young man, who threw his right fist at the crouching Carella and suddenly found himself flying over Carella's head to land flat on his back in the sawdust. He did next what he had done instinctively since the time he was twelve years old. He reached for a knife in the side pocket of his trousers. Carella did not wait for the knife to clear his pocket. Carella kicked him cleanly and swiftly in the balls. Then he turned to the bar, where another young man seemed ready to spring into action, and very quietly said, 'I'm a police officer. Let's cool it, huh?'

The second young man cooled it very quickly. The place was very silent now. With his back to the bar, and hoping the bartender would not hit him on the head with a sap or a bottle or both, Carella reached under Fletcher's arms and helped him up.

'You okay?' he said.

'Yes, fine,' Fletcher said.

'Come on.'

He walked Fletcher to the door, moving as swiftly as possible. He fully recognized that his shield afforded little enough protection in a place like this, and all he wanted to do was get the hell out fast. On the street, as they stumbled toward the automobile, he prayed only that they would not be cold-cocked before they got to it.

A half-dozen men came out of the bar just as they climbed into the automobile. 'Lock that door!' Carella snapped, and then turned the ignition key, and stepped on the gas, and the car lurched away from the curb in a squeal of burning rubber. He did not ease up on the accelerator until they were a mile from Quigley's, by which time he was certain they were not being followed.

'That was very nice,' Fletcher said.

'Yes, very nice indeed,' Carella said.

'I admire that. I admire a man who can do that,' Fletcher said.

'Why in hell did you pick *that* sweet dive?' Carella asked.

'I wanted you to see them all,' Fletcher said, and then eased his head back against the seat cushion, and fell promptly asleep.

11

Early Monday morning, on Kling's day off, he called Cindy Forrest. It was only seven-thirty, but he knew her sleeping and waking habits as well as he knew his own, and since the phone was on the kitchen wall near the refrigerator, and since she would at that moment be preparing breakfast, he was not surprised when she answered it on the second ring.

'Hello?' she said. She sounded rushed, a trifle breathless. She always allowed herself a scant half hour to get out of the apartment each morning, rushing from bedroom to kitchen to bathroom to bedroom again, finally running for the elevator, looking miraculously well-groomed and sleek and rested and ready to do battle with the world. He visualized her standing now at the kitchen phone, only partially clothed, and felt a faint stirring of desire.

'Hi. Cindy,' he said, 'it's me.'

'Oh, hello, Bert,' she said. 'Can you hold just a second? The coffee's about to boil over.' He waited. In the promised second, she was back on the line. 'Okay,' she said. 'I tried to reach you the other night.'

'Yes, I know. I'm returning your call.'

'Right, right,' she said. There was a long silence. 'I'm trying to remember why I called you. Oh, yes. I found a shirt of yours in the dresser, and I wanted to know what I should do with it. So I called you at home, and there was no answer, and then I figured you probably had night duty, and I tried the squadroom, but Steve said you weren't on. So I decided to wrap it up and mail it. I've already got it all addressed and everything.'

There was another silence.

'So I guess I'll drop it off at the post office on my way to work this morning,' Cindy said.

'Okay,' Kling said.

'If that's what you want me to do,' Cindy said.

'Well, what would you *like* to do?'

'It's all wrapped and everything, so I guess that's what I'll do.'

'Be a lot of trouble to *un*wrap it, I guess,' Kling said.

'Why would I want to unwrap it?'

'I don't know. Why did you call me Saturday night?'

'To ask what you wanted me to do with the shirt.'

'What choices did you have in mind?'

'When? Saturday night?'

'Yes,' Kling said. 'When you called.'

'Well, there were several possibilities, I guess. You could have stopped here to pick up the shirt, or I could have dropped it off at your place or the squadroom, or we could have had a drink together or something, at which time . . .'

'I didn't know that was permissible.'

'Which?'

'Having a drink together. Or *any* of those things, in fact.'

'Well, it's all academic now, isn't it? You weren't home when I called, and you weren't working, either, so I wrapped up the goddamn shirt, and I'll mail it to you this morning.'

'What are you sore about?'

'Who's sore?' Cindy said.

'You sound sore.'

'I have to get out of here in twenty minutes and I still haven't had my coffee.'

'Wouldn't want to be late for the hospital,' Kling said. 'Might upset your friend Dr Freud.'

'Ha-ha,' Cindy said mirthlessly.

'How is he, by the way?'

'He's fine, by the way.'

'Good.'

'Bert?'

'Yes, Cindy?'

'Never mind, nothing.'

'What is it?'

'Nothing. I'll put the shirt in the mail. I washed it and ironed it, I hope it doesn't get messed up.'

'I hope not.'

'Good-bye, Bert,' she said, and hung up.

Kling put the receiver back onto its cradle, sighed, and went into the kitchen. He ate a breakfast of grapefruit juice, coffee, and two slices of toast, and then went back into the bedroom and dialed Nora Simonov's number. When he asked her if she would like to have lunch with him, she politely refused, saying she had an appointment with an art director. Fearful of being turned down for dinner as well, he hedged his bet by asking if she'd like to meet him for a drink at about five, five-thirty. She surprised him by saying she would love it, and they agreed to meet at The Oasis, a quiet cocktail lounge in one of the city's oldest hotels, near the western end of Grover Park. Kling went into the bathroom to brush his teeth.

434 North Sixteenth Street was a brownstone within the precinct territory, between Ainsley and Culver avenues. Meyer and Carella found a listing for an L. Kantor in one of the mailboxes downstairs, tried the inner lobby door, found it unlocked, and started up to the fourth floor without ringing

the downstairs bell. They had tried calling the number listed in Sarah's address book, but the telephone company had reported it temporarily out of service. Whether this was true or not was a serious question for debate.

'The Telephone Blues' was a dirge still being sung by most residents of the city, and it was becoming increasingly more difficult these days to know if a phone was busy, out of order, disconnected, temporarily out of service, or stolen in the night by an international band of telephone thieves. The direct-dialing system had been a brilliant innovation, except that after directly dialing the digits necessary to place a call, the caller was more often than not greeted with: (a) silence; (b) a recording; (c) a busy signal, or (d) a series of strange beeps and boops. After trying to direct-dial the same number three or four times, the caller was inevitably reduced to dealing with one or more operators (all of whom sounded as if they were in a trainee program for people with ratings of less than 48 on the Standford-Binet scale of intelligence) and sometimes actually got to talk to the party he was calling. On too many occasions, Carella visualized someone in desperate trouble trying to reach a doctor, a policeman, or a fireman. The police had a number to call for emergency assistance – but what the hell good was the number if you could never get the *phone* to work? Such were Carella's thoughts as he plodded up the four flights to the apartment of Lou Kantor, the third man listed in Sarah's address book.

Meyer knocked on the door. Both men waited. He knocked again.

'Yes?' a woman's voice said. 'Who is it?'

'Police officers,' Meyer answered.

There was a short silence. Then the woman said, 'Just a moment, please.'

'Think he's home?' Meyer whispered.

Carella shrugged. They heard footsteps approaching the

door. Through the closed door, the woman said, 'What do you want?'

'We're looking for Lou Kantor,' Meyer said.

'Why?'

'Routine investigation,' Meyer said.

The door opened a crack, held by a night-chain. 'Let me see your badge,' the woman said. Whatever else they had learned, the citizens of this good city knew that you always asked a cop to show his badge because otherwise he might turn out to be a robber or a rapist or a murderer, and then where were you? Meyer held up his shield. The woman studied it through the narrow opening, and then closed the door again, slipped off the night-chain, and opened the door wide.

'Come in,' she said.

They went into the apartment. The woman closed and locked the door behind them. They were standing in a small, tidy kitchen. Through a doorless doorframe, they could see into the next room, obviously the living room, with two easy chairs, a sofa, a floor lamp, and a television set. The woman was perhaps thirty-five years old, five feet eight inches tall, with a solid frame, and a square face fringed with short dark hair. She was wearing a robe over pajamas, and she was barefoot. Her eyes were blue and suspicious. She looked from one cop to the other, waiting.

'Is he here?' Meyer asked.

'Is who here?'

'Mr Kantor.'

The woman looked at him, puzzled. Understanding suddenly flashed in her blue eyes. A thin smile formed on her mouth. '*I'm* Lou Kantor,' she said. 'Louise Kantor. What can I do for you?'

'Oh,' Meyer said, and studied her.

'What can I do for you?' Lou repeated. The smile had vanished from her mouth; she was frowning again.

Carella took the photostat from his notebook, and handed it to her. 'Do you know this woman?' he asked.

'Yes,' Lou said.

'Do you know her name?'

'Yes,' Lou said wearily. 'That's Sadie Collins. What about her?'

Carella decided to play it straight. 'She's been murdered,' he said.

'Mmm,' Lou said, and handed the stat back to him. 'I thought so.'

'What made you think so?'

'I saw her picture in the newspaper last week. Or at least a picture of somebody who looked a hell of a lot like her. The name was different, and I told myself, No, it isn't her, but Jesus, there was her picture staring up at me, it *had* to be her.' Lou shrugged and then walked to the stove. 'You want some coffee?' she asked. 'I'll get some going, if you like.'

'Thank you, no,' Carella said. 'How well did you know her, Miss Kantor?'

Lou shrugged again. 'I only knew her a short while. I met her in, I guess it was September. Saw her three or four times after that.'

'Where'd you meet her?' Carella asked.

'In a bar called The Purple Chairs,' Lou answered. 'That's right,' she added quickly, 'that's what I am.'

'Nobody asked,' Carella said.

'Your *eyes* asked.'

'What about Sadie Collins?'

'What about her? Spell it out, officer, I'm not going to help you.'

'Why not?'

'Mainly because I don't like being hassled.'

'Nobody's hassling you, Miss Kantor. You practice your religion and I'll practice mine. We're here to talk about a dead woman.'

'Then talk about her, spit it out. What do you want to know? Was she straight? Everybody's straight until they're *not* straight anymore, isn't that right? She was willing to learn. I taught her.'

'Did you know she was married?'

'I knew. So what?'

'She told you?'

'She told me. Broke down in tears one night, lay in my arms all night crying. I knew she was married.'

'What'd she say about her husband?'

'Nothing that surprised me.'

'What, exactly?'

'She said he had another woman. Said he ran off to see her every weekend, told little Sadie he had out-of-town business. *Every* goddamn weekend, can you imagine that?'

'How long had it been going on?'

'Who knows? She found out about it just before Christmas last year.'

'How often did you say you saw her?'

'Three or four times. She used to come here on weekends, when he was away. Sauce for the goose.'

'What do you make of this?' Carella said, and handed her Sarah's address book, opened to the MEMORANDA page.

'I don't know any of these people,' Lou said.

'The initials under your name,' Carella said.

'Mmm. What about them?'

'TPC and then TG. Got any ideas?'

'Well, the TPC is obvious, isn't it?'

'Obvious?' Carella said.

'Sure. I met her at The Purple Chairs,' Lou said. 'What else could it mean?'

Carella suddenly felt very stupid. 'Of course,' he said, 'what else could it mean?'

'How about those other initials?' Meyer said.

'Haven't the faintest,' Lou answered, and handed back the book. 'Are you finished with me?'

'Yes, thank you very much,' Carella said.

'I miss her,' Lou said suddenly. 'She was a wild one.'

Cracking a code is like learning to roller-skate; once you know how to do it, it's easy. With a little help from Gerald Fletcher, who had provided a guided tour the night before, and with a lot of help from Lou Kantor, who had generously provided the key, Carella was able to study the list in Sarah's book and crack the code wide open. Well, *almost* wide open.

Andrew Hart
1120 Hall Avenue
622 - 8400
   (PB+G) (TG)

Michael Thornton
371 South Lindner
881- 9371
     (TS)

Lou Kantor
434 North 16 Street
FR 7 - 2346
   (TPC) (TG)

Sal Decotto
831 Grover Avenue
FR5 - 3287
   (F) (TG)

Richard Fenner
110 Henderson
693 - 6648
   (QR) (TG)

Last night, Fletcher had taken him, in geographical rather than numerical order, to Paddy's Bar & Grille (PB&G), Fanny's (F), The Purple Chairs (TPC), and Quigley's Rest (QR). For some reason, perhaps to avoid duplication, Sarah Fletcher had felt it necessary to list in code the places in which she had met her various bedmates. It seemed obvious to Carella, now that he knew how to roller-skate, that the TS beneath Michael Thornton's telephone number was meant to indicate nothing more than The Saloon, where Thornton had admitted first meeting her. Gerald Fletcher had not taken Carella there last night, but perhaps the place had been on his itinerary, with the scheduled stop preempted by his own drunkenness and the fight in Quigley's Rest.

But what the hell did TG mean?

By Carella's own modest estimate, he had been in more damn bars in the past twenty-four hours than he had in the past twenty-four years. But he decided nonetheless to hit The Saloon that night. You never learned anything if you didn't ask, and there were imponderables even in roller-skating.

Three wandering violinists moved from table to table playing a medley of 'Ebb Tide,' 'Strangers in the Night,' and 'Where or When,' none of which seemed to move Nora as much as 'Something' had. Fake potted palms dangled limpid plastic fronds while a small pool, honoring the name of the place, gushed before a painted backdrop of desert sand and sky.

'I'm glad you called,' Nora said. 'I hate to go straight home after the end of a busy day. The apartment always feels so empty. And the meeting today was a disaster. The art director is a man who started in the stockroom forty years ago, after a correspondence course from one of those schools that advertise on matchbook covers. So he had the gall to tell me what was wrong with the girl's hand.' She looked up from her drink and said, in explanation, 'It was this drawing of a girl, with her hand sort of brushing a strand of hair away from her cheek.'

'I see,' Kling said.

'Do *you* have to put up with that kind of crap?' she asked.

'Sometimes.'

'Anyway, I'm glad you called. There's nothing like a drink after a session with a moron.'

'How about the company?'

'What?'

'I'm glad you appreciate the drink . . .'

'Oh, stop it,' Nora said, 'you *know* I like the company.'

'Since when?'

'Since always. Now just cut it out.'

'May I ask you something?'

'Sure.'

'Why are you here with me, instead of your boyfriend?'

'Well,' Nora said, and turned away preparatory to lying, 'as I told you . . . oh, *look*, the violinists are coming over. Think of a request, quick.'

'Ask them to play "Something,"' Kling said, and Nora turned back toward him immediately, her eyes flashing.

'That isn't funny, Bert,' she said.

'Tell me about your boyfriend.'

'There's nothing to tell you. He's a doctor and he spends a lot of time in his office and at the hospital. As a result, he's not always free when I'd like him to be, and, therefore, I felt it perfectly all right to have a drink with you. In fact, if you wouldn't be so smart all the time, saying I should request "Something" when you know the song has particular meaning for me, you *might* ask me to have dinner with you, and I might possibly say "yes."'

'*Would* you like to have dinner with me?' Kling asked, astonished.

'Yes,' Nora said.

'There isn't a boyfriend at all, is there?' he said.

'Don't make that mistake, Bert. There *is* one, and I love him. And I'm going to marry him as soon as . . .' She cut herself short, and turned away again.

'As soon as *what*?' Kling asked.

'Here are the violinists,' Nora said.

One storm had blown out to sea, but another was approaching, and this time it looked as though the forecasters would be right. The first flakes had not yet begun to fall as Carella walked up the street toward The Saloon, but snow was in the air, you could smell it, you could sense it, the goddamn city would be a frozen tundra by morning. Carella did not particularly like snow. His one brief romance with it had been, oh, several years ago, when some punk arsonists had set fire to him (talk about Dick Tracy!) and he had put out the flames by rolling in a bank of the stuff. But how long can any hot love affair last? Not very. Carella's disaffection had begun again the very next week, when it again snowed, and he again slipped and slogged and sloshed along with ten million other winter-weary citizens of the city. He looked up at the sky now, pulled a sour face, and went inside.

The Saloon was just that: a saloon.

A cigarette-scarred bar behind which ran a mottled, flaking mirror. Wooden booths with patched leatherette seat cushions. Bowls of pretzels and potato chips. Jukebox bubbling and gurgling, rock music babbling and bursting, the smell of steamy bodies and steamy garments, the incessant rise and fall of too many voices talking too loud. He hung his coat on the sagging rack near the cigarette machine, found himself a relatively uncrowded spot at the far end of the bar, and ordered a beer. Because of the frantic activity behind and in front of the bar, he knew it would be quite some while before he could catch the bartender's ear. As it turned out, he did not actually get to talk to him until eleven-thirty, at which time the business of drinking yielded to the more serious business of trying to make out.

'They come in here,' the bartender said, 'at all hours of the night, each and every one of them looking for the same thing. Relentless. You know what that word means? Relentless? That's what the action is here.'

'Yeah, it is kind of frantic,' Carella said.

'Frantic? That's the word, all right. Frantic. Men and women both. Mostly men. The women come for the same thing, you understand? But it takes a lot more fortitude for a woman to go in a bar alone, even if it's *this* kind of place where the only reason anybody comes at all is to meet people, you understand? Fortitude. You know what that word means? Fortitude?'

'Yeah,' Carella said, and nodded.

'Take yourself,' the bartender said. 'You're here to meet a girl, am I right?'

'I'm here mostly to have a few beers and relax,' Carella said.

'Relax? With *that* music? You could just as easy relax in World War II, on the battlefield. Were you in World War II?'

'Yes, I was,' Carella said.

'That was *some* war,' the bartender said. 'The wars they got nowadays are bullshit wars. But World War II?' He grinned fondly and appreciatively. '*That* was a *glorious* war! You know what that word means? Glorious?'

'Yeah,' Carella said.

'Excuse me, I got a customer down the other end,' the bartender said, and walked off. Carella sipped at his beer. Through the plate-glass window facing the side street, he could see the first snowflakes beginning to fall. Great, he thought, and looked at his watch.

The bartender mixed and served the drink, and then came back. 'What'd you do in the war?' he asked.

'Goof off, mostly,' Carella said, and smiled.

'No, seriously. Be serious.'

'I was in the Infantry,' Carella said.

'Who wasn't? Did you get overseas?'

'Yes.'

'Where?'

'Italy.'

'See any action?'

'A little,' Carella said. 'Listen . . . getting back to the idea of meeting somebody . . .'

'In here, it *always* gets back to that.'

'There *was* someone I was hoping to see.'

'Who?' the bartender said.

'A girl named Sadie Collins.'

'Yeah,' the bartender said, and nodded.

'Do you know her?'

'Yeah.'

'Have you seen her around lately?'

'No. She used to come in a lot, but I ain't seen her in months. What do you want to fool around with her for?'

'Why? What's the matter with her?'

'You want to know something?' the bartender said. 'I thought she was a hooker at first. I almost had her thrown out. The boss don't like hookers hanging around here.'

'What made you think she was a hooker?'

'Aggressive. You know what that word means? Aggressive? She used to come dressed down to here and up to here, which is pretty far out, even compared to some of the things they're wearing today. She was ready for action, you understand? She was selling everything she had.'

'Well, most women try to . . .'

'No, no, this wasn't like *most* women, don't give me that

most women crap. She'd come in here, pick out a guy she wanted, and go after him like the world was gonna end at midnight. All business, just like a hooker, except she wasn't charging. Knew just what she wanted, and went straight for it, *bam*. And I could always tell *exactly* who she was gonna end up with, even before she knew it herself.'

'How could you tell?'

'Always the same type.'

'What type?'

'Big guys, first of all. You wouldn't stand a chance with her, you're lucky she ain't here. Not that you ain't big, don't misunderstand me. But Sadie liked them gigantic. You know what that word means? Gigantic? That was Sadie's type. Gigantic and mean. All I had to do was look around the room and pick out the biggest, meanest son of a bitch in the place, and that's who Sadie would end up with. You want to know something?'

'What?'

'I'm glad she don't come in here anymore. She used to make me nervous. There was something about her . . . don't know.' The bartender shook his head. 'Like she was compulsive. You know what that word means? Compulsive?'

He had left Nora at the door to her apartment, where she had given him her customary handshake and her now-expected 'Thank you, I had a very nice time,' and rode down in the elevator now, wondering what his next move should be. He did not believe her doctor-boyfriend existed (he seemed to be having a lot of trouble lately with girls and their goddamn doctor-boyfriends) but at the same time he accepted the fact that there *was* a man in her life, a flesh-and-blood person whose identity, for some bewildering reason, Nora chose not to reveal. Kling did not appreciate anonymous competition. He wondered if a *blitz* might not be in order, telephone call when he got back to his apartment, another call in the morning, a dozen roses, a telegram, another dozen calls, another dozen roses, the whole stupid adolescent barrage, all of it designed to convince a girl that somebody out there was madly in love with her.

He wondered if he was madly in love with her.

He decided he was not.

Then why was he expending all this energy? He recalled reading someplace that when a man and a woman got divorced, it was usually the man who remarried first. He supposed that what he had shared with Cindy was a marriage, of sorts, and the sudden termination of it . . . well, it was silly to think of it in terms of a marriage. But he supposed the end of it (and it certainly seemed to have ended) *could* be considered a divorce, of sorts. In which case, his frantic pursuit of Nora was merely a part of the reaction syndrome, and . . .

Damn it, he thought. Hang around with a psychologist long enough and you begin to sound like one.

He stepped out of the elevator, walked swiftly through the lobby, and came out of the building into a blinding snowstorm. It had not been this bad ten minutes ago, when the taxi had dropped them off. The snow was thick and fast now, the wind blowing it in angry swirls that lashed his face and flicked away, successively, incessantly. He ducked his head, and began walking up toward the lighted avenue at the end of the block, his hands in his pockets. He was on the verge of deciding that he would not try to see Nora Simonov again, would not even call her again, when three men stepped out of a doorway, directly into his path.

He looked up too late.

A fist came out of the flying snow, smashing him full in the face. He staggered back, his hands still in his pockets. Two of the men seized him from behind, grabbing both his arms, his hands still trapped in his pockets. The one standing in front of him smashed a fist into his face again. His head snapped back. He felt blood gushing from his nose. 'Keep away from Nora,' the man whispered, and then began pounding his fists into Kling's abdomen and chest, blow after blow while Kling fought to free his arms and his hands, his strength ebbing, his struggle weakening, slumping as the men behind him held his arms, and the man in front battered relentlessly with short hard jabs until Kling wanted to scream aloud, and then wanted only to die, and then felt the welcome oblivion of unconsciousness and did not know when they released him at last and allowed him to fall face forward into the white snow, bleeding.

12

'All right,' Byrnes said, 'I've got a cop in the hospital, now what the hell happened?'

Tuesday morning sunshine assaulted the lieutenant's corner window. The storm had ended, and the snowplows had come through, and mile-high snowbanks lined the streets, piled against the curb. It was four days before Christmas, and the temperature was below freezing, and unless the city's soot triumphed, the twenty-fifth would still be white.

Arthur Brown was black. Six feet four inches tall, weighing 220 pounds, with the huge frame and powerful muscles of a heavyweight fighter, he stood before the lieutenant's desk, his eyes squinted against the sunshine.

'I thought you were tailing Fletcher,' Byrnes said.

'I was,' Brown answered.

'All right. Fletcher and this girl live in the same goddamn building. Kling was jumped *leaving* the building. If you were on Fletcher . . .'

'I was on him from five o'clock yesterday afternoon, when he left his office downtown.' Brown reached into his inside jacket pocket. 'Here's the timetable,' he said. 'I didn't get back to Silvermine Oval till after midnight. By that time, they'd already taken Bert to the hospital.'

'Let me see it,' Byrnes said, and took the typewritten sheet from Brown's hand, and silently studied it:

SURVEILLANCE GERALD FLETCHER
Monday, December 20

4:55 P.M.-Relieved Detective Kapek outside office bldg 4400 Butler. Suspect emerged 5:10 P.M., went to his car parked in local garage, and drove to home at 721 Silvermine Oval, entered bldg at 5:27 P.M.

7:26 P.M.-Suspect emerged from building, started to walk south, came back, talked to doorman, and waited for his car. Drove to 812 North Crane, parked. Suspect entered apartment building there at 8:04 P.M.

8:46 P.M.-Suspect emerged from 812 North Crane in company of redheaded woman wearing fur coat (black) and green dress, green shoes, approx height and weight five-six, 120, approx age thirty. Drove to Rudolph's Restaurant, 127 Harrow. Surveillant (black) tried to get table, was told he needed reservations, went outside to wait in sedan. 9:05 P.M.

Byrnes looked up. 'What's this crap about needing a reservation? Was the place crowded?'
'No, but . . .'
'Anything we can nail them on, Artie?'
'Just try to prove anything,' Brown said.
'Stupid pricks,' Byrnes said, and went back to the timetable.

10:20 P.M.-Suspect and redheaded woman came out of Rudolph's, drove back to 812 Crane, arrived 10:35

P.M., went into building. No doorman, surveillant entered unobserved, elevator indicator stopped at eleventh floor. Check of lobby mailboxes showed eight apartments on eleventh floor (names of occupants not marked as to color of hair).

Byrnes looked up again, sharply this time. Brown grinned. Byrnes went back to the report, sighing.

11:40 P.M.-Suspect came out of building, walked north to Glade, where he had parked car, and drove directly home, arriving there ten minutes past midnight. 721 Silvermine scene of great activity, two RMP cars in street, patrolman questioning doorman. Suspect said few words to doorman, then went inside. Detective Bob O'Brien already on scene and waiting to relieve, reported Kling had been assaulted half hour ago and taken to Culver Avenue Hospital. Relieved by O'Brien at 12:15 A.M.

'When did O'Brien get there?' Byrnes asked.

'I radioed in when I was leaving the woman's building, told O'Brien the suspect was probably heading home, and asked him to relieve me there. He said he arrived a little after midnight. The ambulance had already come and gone.'

'How's Bert?' Byrnes asked.

'I checked a few minutes ago. He's conscious, but they're holding him for observation.'

'He say anything?'

'Three guys jumped him,' Brown said.

'Sons of bitches,' Byrnes said.

Carella had not yet spoken to either Sal Decotto or Richard Fenner, the two remaining people listed in Sarah's book, but he saw no reason to pursue that trail any further. He had been taken to the bars where Sarah (or rather Sadie) had picked them up, and whereas he was not the type of person who ordinarily judged a book by its cover, he had a fair idea of what the men themselves would be like. Big and mean, according to the bartender at The Saloon.

The hardest thing Carella had ever had to learn in his entire life was that there actually *were* mean people in the world. As a young man, he had always believed that people behaved badly only because they'd experienced unhappy childhoods or unfortunate love affairs or deaths in the family or any one of a hundred assorted traumas. He changed his mind about that when he began working for the Police Department. He learned then that there were good people doing bad things, and there were also mean rotten bastards doing bad things. The good ones ended in jail just as easily as the mean ones, but the mean ones were the ones to beware. Why Sarah Fletcher had sought out big, mean men (and apparently one mean woman as well) was anybody's guess. If the place-listings in her book could be considered chronological, she'd gone from bad to worse in her search for partners, throwing in a solitary dyke for good measure (or was Sal Decotto a woman, too?), and ending up at Quigley's Rest, which was no afternoon tea party.

But why? To give it back to her husband in spades? If *he* was playing around with someone each and every weekend, maybe Sarah decided to beat him at his own game, become not only Sadie, but a Sadie who was, in the words of her various admirers, 'a crazy bitch,' 'a stupid swat,' and 'a wild one.' It seemed entirely possible that the only thing Carella would learn from Richard Fenner or Sal Decotto was that they shared identical opinions of the woman they had similarly used and abused. And affirmation of a conclusion leading nowhere was a waste of time. Carella tossed Sarah's little black book into the manila folder bearing the various reports on the case, and turned his attention to the information Artie Brown had brought in last night.

Cherchez la femme was a handy little dictum perhaps used more often by the *Sûreté* than by the 87th. But without trying to *cherche* any *femme*, Brown had inadvertently come across one anyway, a thirty-year-old redhead who lived on the eleventh floor at 812 North Crane and with whom Gerald Fletcher had spent almost four hours the night before. It would have been a simple matter to hit the redhead's building and find out exactly who she was, but Carella decided against such a course of action. A chat with the superintendent, however quiet, a questioning of neighbors, however discreet, might get back to the woman herself, and serve to alert Fletcher. Fletcher was the suspect. Carella sometimes had to remind himself of that fact. Sarah had been playing around with an odd assortment of men and women, five according to her own record (and God knew how many more she had not listed, and God knew what the 'TG' after four of the names meant); her blatant infidelity provided Fletcher with a strong motive, despite his own weekend sorties into realms as yet uncharted. So why take Carella to his wife's unhappy haunts, why *show* Carella that he had good and sufficient reason to rip that knife across her belly? And why the hell offer to get a good defense attorney for the boy who had already been indicted for the slaying and who, unless somebody came up with something concrete damn soon, might very well be convicted of the crime?

Sometimes Carella wondered who was doing what to whom.

At five o'clock that evening, he relieved Detective Hal Willis outside Fletcher's office building downtown, and then followed Fletcher to a department store in midtown Isola. Carella did not normally go in for cops-and-robbers disguises, but Fletcher knew exactly what he looked like and so he was wearing a false mustache stuck to his upper lip with spirit gum, a wig with longer hair than his own and of a different color (a dirty blond whereas his own was brown), and a pair of sunglasses. The disguise, he was certain, would not have fooled Fletcher at close range. But he did not intend to get that close, and he felt pretty secure he would not be made. He was, in fact, more nervous about *losing* Fletcher than about being spotted by him.

The store was thronged with late shoppers. This was Tuesday, December 21, four days to the big one, only three more days of shopping once the stores closed tonight at nine. Hot desperation flowed beneath the cool white plastic icicles that hung from the ceiling, panic in wonderland, the American anxiety syndrome never more evident than at Christmas, when the entire nation became a ruthless jackpot – Two Hundred Million Neediest gifting and getting, with a gigantic hangover waiting just around the new year's corner. Gerald Fletcher shoved through the crowd of holiday shoppers like a quarterback moving the ball downfield without benefit of blockers. Carella, like a reticent tackler, followed some twenty feet behind.

The elevator would be a danger spot. Carella saw the elevator bank at the far end of the store, and knew that Fletcher was heading directly for it, and weighed the chances of being spotted in a crowded car against the chances of losing Fletcher if he did not follow immediately on his heels. He did not know how many thousands of people were in the store at that moment; he *did* know that if he allowed Fletcher to get into an elevator without him, the surveillance was blown. The elevator would stop at every floor, the way most department-store elevators did, and Fletcher could get out at any one of them, *then* try to find him again.

An elevator arrived. Its door opened, and Fletcher waited

while the passengers disembarked and then stepped into the car together with half a dozen shoppers. Carella ungentlemanly shoved his way past a woman in a leopard coat and got into the car with his back to Fletcher, who was standing against the rear wall. The car, as Carella had surmised, stopped at every floor. He studiously kept his back to the rear of the car, moving aside whenever anyone wanted to get out. On the fifth floor, he heard Fletcher call, 'Getting out, please,' and then felt him coming toward the front of the car, and saw him stepping out, and waited for the count of three before he, himself, moved forward, much to the annoyance of the elevator operator, who was starting to close the door.

Fletcher had walked off to the left. Carella spotted him moving swiftly up one of the aisles, looking about at the signs identifying each of the various departments, and stopping at one marked INTIMATE APPAREL. Carella walked into the next aisle over, pausing to look at women's robes and kimonos, keeping one eye on Fletcher, who was in conversation with the lingerie salesgirl. The girl nodded, smiled, and showed him what appeared to be either a slip or a short nightgown, holding the garment up against her ample bosom to model it for Fletcher, who nodded, and said something else to her. The girl disappeared under the counter, to reappear several moments later, her hands overflowing with gossamer undergarments, which she spread on the counter before Fletcher, awaiting his further choice.

'May I help you, sir?' a voice said, and Carella turned to find a stocky woman at his elbow, gray hair, black-rimmed spectacles, wearing army shoes and a black dress with a small white collar. She looked exactly like a prison matron, right down to the suspicious smile that silently accused him of being a junkie shoplifter or worse.

'Thank you, no,' Carella said. 'I'm just looking.'

Fletcher was making his selections, pointing now to this

garment, now to another. The salesgirl wrote up the order, and Fletcher reached into his wallet to give her either cash or a credit card, it was diffcult to tell from this distance. He chatted with the girl a moment longer, and then walked off toward the elevator bank.

'Are you *sure* I can't assist you?' the prison matron said, and Carella immediately answered, 'I'm positive,' and moved swiftly toward the lingerie counter. Fletcher had left the counter without a package in his arms, which meant he was *sending* his purchases. You did not send dainty underthings to a prize fighter, and Carella wanted very much to know exactly which woman was to be the recipient of the 'intimate apparel.' The salesgirl was already gathering up Fletcher's selections – a black half-slip, a wildly patterned Pucci chemise, a peach-colored baby-doll nightgown with matching bikini panties, and four other pairs of panties, blue, black, white, and beige, each trimmed with lace around the legholes. The girl looked up.

'Yes, sir,' she said, 'may I help you?'

Carella opened his wallet and produced his shield. 'Police officer,' he said. 'I'm interested in the order you just wrote up.'

The girl was perhaps nineteen years old, a college girl working in the store for the Christmas rush. The most exciting thing that had happened on the job, until this very moment, was an elderly Frenchman asking her if she would like to spend the month of February on his yacht in the Mediterranean. Speechlessly, the girl studied the shield, her eyes bugging. It suddenly occurred to Carella that Fletcher might have had the purchases sent to his home address, in which case all this undercover work was merely a waste of time. Well, he thought, you win some, you lose some.

'Are these items being sent?' he asked.

'Yes, *sir*,' the girl said. Her eyes were still wide behind her glasses. She wet her lips and stood up a little straighter, prepared to be a perfect witness.

'Can you tell me where?' Carella asked.

'Yes, *sir*,' she said, and turned the sales slip toward him. 'He wanted them wrapped separately, but they're all going to the same address. Miss Arlene Orton, 812 Crane Street, right here in the city.'

'Thank you very much,' Carella said.

It felt like Christmas Day already.

Bert Kling was sitting up in bed and polishing off his dinner when Carella got to the hospital at close to 7 P.M. The men shook hands, and Carella took a seat by the bed.

'This stuff tastes awful,' Kling said, 'but I've been hungry as hell, ever since I got in here. I could almost eat the tray.'

'When are you getting out?'

'Tomorrow morning. I've got a broken rib, nice, huh?'

'Very nice,' Carella said.

'I'm lucky they didn't mess up my insides,' Kling said. 'That's what the doctors were afraid of, internal hemorrhaging. But I'm okay, it seems. They taped up the rib, and whereas I won't be able to do my famous trapeze act for a while, I should be able to get around.'

'Who did it, Bert?'

'Three locomotives, it felt like.'.

'Why?'

'A warning to stay away from Nora Simonov.'

'Were you seeing a lot of her?'

'I saw her twice. Apparently someone saw me seeing her. And decided to put me in the hospital. Little did they know I'm a minion of the law, huh?'

'Little did they know,' Carella said.

'I'll have to ask Nora a few questions when I get out of here. How's the case going?'

'I've located Fletcher's girlfriend.'

'I didn't know he had one.'

'Brown tailed them last night, got an address for her, but no name. Fletcher just sent her some underwear.'

'Nice,' Kling said.

'Very nice. I'm getting a court order to put a wire in the apartment.'

'What do you expect them to talk about?'

'Bloody murder maybe,' Carella said, and shrugged. Both men were silent for several moments.

'You know what I want for Christmas?' Kling asked suddenly.

'What?'

'I want to find those guys who beat me up.'

13

The man who picked the lock on Arlene Orton's front door, ten minutes after she left her apartment on Wednesday morning, was better at it than any burglar in the city, and he happened to work for the Police Department. He had the door open in three minutes flat, at which time a technician went in and wired the joint. It took the technician longer to set up his equipment than it had taken his partner to open the door, but both were artists in their own right, and the sound man had a lot more work to do.

The telephone was the easiest of his jobs. He unscrewed the carbon mike in the mouthpiece of the phone, replaced it with his own mike, attached his wires, screwed the mouthpiece back on, and was instantly in business – or almost in business. The tap would not become operative until the telephone company supplied the police with a list of so-called bridging points that located the pairs and cables for Arlene Orton's phone. The monitoring equipment would be hooked into these, and whenever a call went out of or came into the apartment, a recorder would automatically tape both ends of the conversation. In addition, whenever a call was made from the apartment, a dial indicator would ink out a series of dots that signified the number being called. The police listener would be monitoring the equipment from wherever the bridging point happened to be; in Arlene Orton's case, the location index was seven blocks away.

The technician, while he had Arlene's phone apart, could just as easily have installed a bug that would have picked up any voices in the living room and would also have recorded Arlene's half of any telephone conversations. He chose instead to place his bug in the bookcase on the opposite side of the room. The bug was a small FM transmitter with a battery-powered mike that needed to be changed every twenty-four hours. It operated on the same frequency as the recording machine locked into it, a machine that was voice-actuated and that would begin taping whenever anyone began speaking in the apartment. The technician would have preferred running his own wires, rather than having to worry about changing a battery every twenty-four hours. But running wires meant that you had to pick a place to run them *to*, usually following electrical or telephone circuits to an empty apartment or closet or what-have-you where a policeman would monitor the recording equipment. If a tap was being set up in a hotel room, it was usually possible to rent the room next door, put your listener into it, and go about your messy business without anyone being the wiser. But in this city, empty apartments were about as scarce as working telephones, and whereas the wire was being installed by court order, the technician dared not ask the building superintendent for an empty closet or a workroom in which to hide his listener. Building supers are perhaps not as garrulous as barbers, but the effectiveness of a wiretap is directly proportionate to the secrecy surrounding it, and a blabbermouth superintendent can kill an investigation more quickly than a squad of gangland goons.

So the technician settled upon the battery-powered mike and resigned himself to the fact that every twenty-four hours he and his partner would have to get into the apartment somehow to change the goddamn batteries. In all, there would be four sets of batteries to change because the technician was planting four bugs in the apartment: one in the kitchen, one in the bedroom, one in the bathroom, and one in the living room. While he worked, his partner was down in the lobby with a walkie-talkie in his coat pocket, ready to let him know the moment Arlene Orton came back to the building, and ready to detain her by ruse if necessary. Watching the clock, the technician worked swiftly and silently, hoping the walkie-talkie clipped to his belt would not erupt with his partner's warning voice. He was not worried about legal action against the city; the court order, in effect, gave him permission to break and enter. He worried only about blowing the surveillance.

In the rear of a panel truck parked at the curb some twelve feet south of the entrance to 812 Crane, Steve Carella sat behind the recording equipment that was locked into the frequency of the four bugs. He knew that in some neighborhoods a phony truck was as readily recognizable as the cop on the beat. Put a man in the back of a fake delivery truck, park the truck on the street and start taking pictures of people going in and out of a candy store suspected of being a numbers drop, and all of a sudden the neighborhood was full of budding stars and starlets, all of whom knew there was a cop-photographer in the back of the truck, all of whom mugged and pranced and emoted shamelessly for the movie camera, while managing to conduct not an iota of business that had anything at all to do with the policy racket. It got discouraging. But Crane Street was in one of the city's better neighborhoods, where perhaps the citizens were not as wary of cops hiding in the backs of panel trucks doing their dirty watching and listening. Carella sat hopefully with a tuna-fish sandwich and a bottle of beer, prepared to hear and record any sounds that emanated from Arlene's apartment.

At the bridging point seven blocks away and thirty minutes later, Arthur Brown sat behind equipment that was hooked into the telephone mike, and waited for Arlene Orton's phone to ring. He was in radio contact with Carella in the back of his phony panel truck and could apprise him of any new development at once.

The first call came at 12:17 P.M. The equipment tripped in automatically, and the spools of tape began recording the conversation while Brown simultaneously monitored it through his headphones.

'Hello?'

'Hello, Arlene?'

'Yes, who's this?'

'Nan.'

'Nan? You sound so different. Do you have a cold or something?'

'Every year at this time. Just before the holidays. Arlene, I'm terribly rushed, I'll make this short. Do you know Beth's dress size?'

'A ten, I would guess. Or an eight.'

'Well, which?'

'I don't know. Why don't you give Danny a ring?'

'Do you have his office number?'

'No, but he's listed. It's Reynolds and Abelman. In Calm's Point.'

'Thank you, darling. Let's have lunch after the holidays sometime, okay?'

'Love to.'

'I'll call you. Bye-bye.'

Arlene Orton spoke to three more girlfriends in succession. The first one was intent on discussing, among other things, a new birth-control pill she was trying. Arlene told her that she, herself, had stopped taking the pill after her divorce. In the beginning, the very thought of sex was abhorrent to her, and since she had no intention of even *looking* at another man for as long as she lived, she saw no reason to be taking the pill. Later on, when she revised her estimate of the opposite sex, her doctor asked her to stay off the pill for a while. Her friend wanted to know what Arlene was using now, and they went into a long and detailed conversation about the effectiveness of diaphragms, condoms, and intrauterine coils. Brown never did find out what Arlene was using now. Arlene's second girlfriend had just returned from Granada, and she gave a long and breathless report on the hotel at which she'd stayed, mentioning in passing that the tennis pro had great legs. Arlene said that she had not played tennis in three years because tennis had been her former husband's sport, and anything that reminded her of him caused her to throw up violently. Arlene's third girlfriend talked exclusively about a nude stage show she had seen downtown the night before, stating flatly that it was the filthiest thing she had ever seen in her life, and you know me, Arlene, I'm certainly no prude.

Arlene then called the local supermarket to order the week's groceries (including a turkey, which Brown assumed was for Christmas Day), and then called the credit department of one of the city's bigger department stores to complain that she had left a valise with the superintendent for return to the store, but that the new man they had doing pickups and delivery was an absolute idiot, and the valise had been sitting there in the super's apartment for the past three weeks, and thank God she hadn't planned on taking a trip or anything because the suitcase she ordered to *replace* the one she was returning *still* hadn't been delivered, and she felt this was disgraceful in view of the fact that she had spent something like $2000 at the store this year and was now reduced to arguing with a goddamn computer.

She had a fine voice, Arlene Orton, deep and forceful,

punctuated every so often (when she was talking to her girlfriends) with a delightful giggle that seemed to bubble up from some adolescent spring. Brown enjoyed listening to her.

At 4 P.M. the telephone in Arlene's apartment rang again.

'Hello?'

'Arlene, this is Gerry.'

'Hello, darling.'

'I'm leaving here a little early, I thought I'd come right over.'

'Good.'

'Miss me?'

'Mmm-huh.'

'Love me?'

'Mmm-huh.'

'Someone there with you?'

'No.'

'Then why don't you say it?'

'I love you.'

'Good. I'll be there in, oh, half an hour, forty minutes.'

'Hurry.'

Brown radioed Carella at once. Carella thanked him, and sat back to wait.

Standing in the hallway outside Nora Simonov's apartment, Kling wondered what his approach should be. It seemed to him that, where Nora was concerned, he was always working out elaborate strategies. It further seemed to him that any girl for whom you had to draw up detailed battle plans was a girl well worth dropping. He reminded himself that he was not here today on matters of the heart, but rather on matters of the rib – the third rib on the right-hand side of his chest, to be exact. He rang the doorbell and waited. He heard no sound from within the apartment, no footsteps approaching the door, but suddenly the peephole flap was thrown back, and he knew Nora was looking out at him; he raised his right hand, waggled the fingers on it, and grinned. The peephole flap closed again. He heard her unlocking the door. The door opened wide.

'Hi,' she said.

'Hi. I happened to be in the building, checking out some things, and thought I'd stop by to say hello.'

'Come in,' Nora said.

'You're not busy, are you?'

'I'm always busy, but come in, anyway.'

It was the first time he had been allowed entrance to her apartment; maybe she figured he was safe with a broken rib, if indeed she *knew* one of his ribs was broken. There was a spacious entrance foyer opening onto a wide living room. What appeared to be an operative fireplace was on the wall opposite the windows. The room was done in bright, rich colors, the fabric on the easy chairs and sofa subtly echoing the color of the rug and drapes. It was a warm and pleasant room; he would have enjoyed being in it as a person rather than a cop. He thought it supremely ironic that she had let him in too late, and was now wasting hospitality on nothing but a policeman investigating an assault.

'Can I fix you a drink?' she asked. 'Or is it too early for you?'

'I'd love a drink.'

'Name it.'

'What are *you* having?'

'I thought I'd whip up a pitcherful of martinis, and light the cannel coal, and we could sit toasting Christmas.'

'Good idea.' He watched her as she moved toward the bar in the corner of the room. She was wearing work clothes, a paint-smeared white smock over blue jeans. Her dark hair was pulled back, away from her exquisite profile. She moved gracefully and fluidly, walking erect, the way most tall girls did, as though in rebuttal for the years when they'd been forced to slump in order to appear shorter than the tallest boys in the class. She turned and saw him watching her. She smiled, obviously pleased, and said, 'Gin or vodka?'

'Gin.'

He waited until she had taken the gin bottle from behind the bar, and then he said, 'Where's the bathroom, Nora?'

'Down the hall. The very end of it. You mean to tell me cops go to the bathroom, too, the same as mortals?'

He smiled and went out of the room, leaving her busy at the bar. He walked down the long hallway, glancing into the small studio room – drawing board overhung with a fluorescent light, painting of a man jumping up for something, arms stretched over his head, chest muscles rippling, tubes of acrylic paint twisting on a worktable near an empty easel – and continued walking. The bedroom door was open. He looked back toward the living room, closed the bathroom door rather more noisily than was necessary, and stepped quickly into the bedroom.

He went to the dresser first. A silver-framed photograph of a man was on the right-hand end of it. It was inscribed 'To Sweet Nora, with all my love, Frankie.' He studied the man's face, trying to relate it to any of the three men who had jumped him on Monday night. The street had been dark; he had really seen only the one who'd stood in front of him, pounding his fists into his chest and his gut. The man in the photograph was not his attacker. He quickly opened the top drawer of the dresser – panties, nylons, handkerchiefs, brassieres. He closed it, opened the middle drawer, found it full of sweaters and blouses, and then searched the bottom drawer, where Nora kept an odd assortment of gloves, nightgowns, panty-hose, and slips. He closed the drawer and moved rapidly to the night table on the left of the bed, the one upon which the telephone rested. He opened the top drawer, found

Nora's address book, and quickly scanned it. There was only one listing for a man named Frank – Frank Richmond in Calm's Point. Kling closed the book, went to the door, looked down the hallway, and wondered how much more time he had. He stepped across the hall, eased open the bathroom door, closed it behind him, flushed the toilet, and then turned on the cold water tap. He went into the hallway again, closed the door gently behind him, and crossed swiftly into the bedroom again.

He found what he wanted in the night table on the other side of the bed – a stack of some two dozen letters, all on the same stationery, bound together with a thick rubber band. The top envelope in the pile was addressed to Nora at 721 Silvermine Oval. The return address in the left-hand corner of the envelope read:

> Frank Richmond, 80–17–42
> Castleview State Penitentiary
> Castleview-on-Rawley, 23751

Whatever else Frank Richmond was, he was also a convict. Kling debated putting the letters back into the night-table drawer, decided he wanted to read them, and stuck them instead into the right-hand pocket of his jacket. He closed the drawer, went across the hall to the bathroom, turned off the water tap, and went back into the living room, where Nora had started a decent fire and was pouring the drinks.

'Find it?' she asked.

'Yes,' he answered.

14

On Thursday morning, two days before Christmas, Carella sat at his desk in the squadroom and looked over the transcripts Miscolo's clerical staff had typed up for him. He had taped five reels the night before, beginning at 4:55, when Fletcher had entered Arlene Orton's apartment, and ending at 7:30, when they left to go out to dinner. The reel that interested him most was the second one. The conversation on that reel had at one point changed abruptly in tone and content; Carella thought he knew why, but he wanted to confirm his suspicion by carefully reading the typewritten record:

> The following is a transcript of a conversation between Gerald Fletcher and Arlene Orton which took place in Miss Orton's apartment (11D) at 812 Crane Street on Wednesday, December 22. Conversation on this reel took place commencing at approximately 5:21 P.M. and ended at approximately 5:45 P.M. on that date.

> Fletcher: I meant after the holidays.
> Miss Orton: I thought you meant after the trial.
> Fletcher: No, the holidays.

Miss Orton:	I may be able to get away, I'm not sure. I'll have to check with my shrink.
Fletcher:	What's he got to do with it?
Miss Orton:	Well, I have to pay whether I'm there or not, you know.
Fletcher:	You mean, oh, I see.
Miss Orton:	Sure.
Fletcher:	It would be best if we could . . .
Miss Orton:	Sure, coordinate it if we can.
Fletcher:	Is he taking a vacation?
Miss Orton:	He went in February last time.
Fletcher:	February, right.
Miss Orton:	Two weeks.
Fletcher:	In February, right, I remember.
Miss Orton:	I'll ask him.
Fletcher:	Yes, ask him. Because I'd really like to get away.
Miss Orton:	Ummm. When do you think the case [Inaudible]
Fletcher:	In March sometime. No sooner than that. He's got a new lawyer, you know.
Miss Orton:	Do you want some more of this?
Fletcher:	Just a little.
Miss Orton:	On the cracker or the toast?
Fletcher:	What did I have it on?
Miss Orton:	The cracker.
Fletcher:	Let me try the toast. Mmmm. Did you make this yourself?
Miss Orton:	No, I got it at the deli. What does that mean, a new lawyer?
Fletcher:	Nothing. He'll be convicted anyway.
Miss Orton:	[Inaudible]
Fletcher:	Well.
Miss Orton:	You making another drink?

Fletcher:	I thought . . .
Miss Orton:	What time is the reservation?
Fletcher:	A quarter to eight.
Miss Orton:	Sure, there's time.
Fletcher:	Do you want another one?
Miss Orton:	Just some ice. One ice cube.
Fletcher:	Okay: Is there any more [Inaudible]
Miss Orton:	Underneath. Did you look underneath?
Fletcher:	[Inaudible]
Miss Orton:	There should be some.
Fletcher:	Yeah, here it is.
Miss Orton:	Thank you.
Fletcher:	Because the trial's going to take a lot out of me.
Miss Orton:	Ummmm.
Fletcher:	I'd like to rest up beforehand.
Miss Orton:	I'll ask him.
Fletcher:	When do you see him again?
Miss Orton:	What's today?
Fletcher:	Wednesday.
Miss Orton:	Tomorrow. I'll ask him then.
Fletcher:	Will he know so far in advance?
Miss Orton:	Well, he'll have some idea.
Fletcher:	Yes, if he can give you at least an approximation . . .
Miss Orton:	Sure, we can plan from there.
Fletcher:	Yes.
Miss Orton:	The trial will be . . . when did you say?
Fletcher:	March. I'm guessing. I think March.
Miss Orton:	How soon after the trial . . .
Fletcher:	I don't know.
Miss Orton:	She's dead, Gerry, I don't see . . .
Fletcher:	Yes, but . . .
Miss Orton:	I don't see any reason to wait, do you?

Fletcher:	No.
Miss Orton:	Then why don't we decide?
Fletcher:	After the trial.
Miss Orton:	Decide after the . . .?
Fletcher:	No, get married after the trial.
Miss Orton:	Yes. But shouldn't we in the meantime . . .
Fletcher:	Have you read this?
Miss Orton:	What is it?
Fletcher:	This.
Miss Orton:	No. I don't like his stuff.
Fletcher:	Then why'd you buy it?
Miss Orton:	I didn't. Maria gave it to me for my birthday. What I was saying, Gerry, is that we ought to set a date now. A provisional date. Depending on when the trial is.
Fletcher::	Mmmm.
Miss Orton:	Allowing ourselves enough time, you know. It'll probably be a long trial, don't you think? Gerry?
Fletcher:	Mmmm?
Miss Orton:	Do you think it'll be a long trial?
Fletcher:	What?
Miss Orton:	Gerry?
Fletcher:	Yes?
Miss Orton:	Where are you?
Fletcher:	I was just looking over some of these books.
Miss Orton:	Do you think you can tear yourself away? So we can discuss . . .
Fletcher:	Forgive me, darling.
Miss Orton:	. . . a matter of some small importance. Like our wedding.

Fletcher:	I'm sorry.
Miss Orton:	If the trial starts in March . . .
Fletcher:	It may or it may not. I told you I was only guessing.
Miss Orton:	Well, say it does start in March.
Fletcher:	If it starts in March . . .
Miss Orton:	How long could it run? At the outside?
Fletcher:	Not very long. A week?
Miss Orton:	I thought murder cases . . .
Fletcher:	Well, they have a confession, the boy's admitted killing her. And there won't be a parade of witnesses, they'll probably call just me and the boy. If it runs longer than a week, I'll be very much surprised.
Miss Orton:	Then if we planned on April . . .
Fletcher:	Unless they come up with something unexpected, of course.
Miss Orton:	Like what?
Fletcher:	Oh, I don't know. They've got some pretty sharp people on this case.
Miss Orton:	In the district attorney's office?
Fletcher:	Investigating it, I mean.
Miss Orton:	What's there to investigate?
Fletcher:	There is always the possibility he didn't do it.
Miss Orton:	Who?
Fletcher:	Corwin. The boy.
Miss Orton:	[Inaudible] a signed confession?
Fletcher:	I thought you didn't want another one?
Miss Orton:	I've changed my mind. [Inaudible] the end of April?
Fletcher:	I guess that would be safe.
Miss Orton:	[Inaudible]

Fletcher:	No, this is fine, thanks.
Miss Orton:	[inaudible] forget about getting away in February. That's when they have hurricanes down there, anyway, isn't it?
Fletcher:	September, I thought. Or October. Isn't that the hurricane season?
Miss Orton:	Go after the trial instead. For our honeymoon.
Fletcher:	They may give me a rough time during the trial.
Miss Orton:	Why should they?
Fletcher:	One of the cops thinks I killed her.
Miss Orton:	You're not serious.
Fletcher:	I am.
Miss Orton:	Who?
Fletcher:	A detective named Carella.
Miss Orton:	Why would he think that?
Fletcher:	Well, he probably knows about us by now . . .
Miss Orton:	How could he?
Fletcher:	He's a very thorough cop. I have a great deal of admiration for him. I wonder if he realizes that.
Miss Orton:	Admiration!
Fletcher:	Yes.
Miss Orton:	Admiration for a man who suspects . . .
Fletcher:	He'd have a hell of a time proving anything, though.
Miss Orton:	Where'd he even get such an idea?
Fletcher:	Well, he knows I hated her.
Miss Orton:	How does he know?
Fletcher:	I told him.
Miss Orton:	What? Gerry, why the hell did you do that?

Fletcher:	Why not?
Miss Orton:	Oh, Gerry.
Fletcher:	He'd have found out anyway. I told you, he's a very thorough cop. He probably knows by now that Sarah was sleeping around with half the men in this city. And he probably knows I knew it, too.
Miss Orton:	That doesn't mean . . .
Fletcher:	If he's also found out about us . . .
Miss Orton:	Who cares what he's found out? Corwin's already confessed. I don't understand you, Gerry.
Fletcher:	I'm only trying to follow his reasoning. Carella's.
Miss Orton:	Is he Italian?
Fletcher:	I would guess so. Why?
Miss Orton:	Italians are the most suspicious people in the world.
Fletcher:	I can understand his reasoning. I'm just not sure he can understand mine.
Miss Orton:	Some reasoning, all right. Why the hell would you kill her? If you were going to kill her, you'd have done it ages ago.
Fletcher:	Of course.
Miss Orton:	When she refused to sign the separation papers.
Fletcher:	Sure.
Miss Orton:	So let him investigate, who cares? You want to know something, Gerry?
Fletcher:	Mmm?
Miss Orton:	Wishing your wife is dead isn't the same thing as killing her. Tell that to Detective Coppola.
Fletcher:	Carella.

Miss Orton:	Carella. Tell him that.
Fletcher:	[Laughs]
Miss Orton:	What's so funny?
Fletcher:	I'll tell him, darling.
Miss Orton:	Good. Meanwhile, the hell with him.
Fletcher:	[Laughs] Do you have to change?
Miss Orton:	I thought I'd go this way. Is it a very dressy place?
Fletcher:	I've never been there.
Miss Orton:	Call them and ask if pants are okay, will you darling?

According to the technician who had wired the Orton apartment, the living-room bug was in the bookcase on the wall opposite the bar. Carella leafed back through the typewritten pages and came upon the section he wanted:

Fletcher:	Have you read this?
Miss Orton:	What is it?
Fletcher:	This.
Miss Orton:	No. I don't like his stuff.
Fletcher:	Then why'd you buy it?
Miss Orton:	I didn't. Maria gave it to me for my birthday. What I was saying, Gerry, is that we ought to set a date now. A provisional date. Depending on when the trial is.
Fletcher:	Mmmm.
Miss Orton:	Allowing ourselves enough time, you know. It'll probably be a long trial, don't you think? Gerry?
Fletcher:	Mmmm?
Miss Orton:	Do you think it'll be a long trial?
Fletcher:	What?

Miss Orton:	Gerry?
Fletcher:	Yes?
Miss Orton:	Where are you?
Fletcher:	I was just looking over some of these books.

It was Carella's guess that Fletcher had discovered the bookcase bug some nine speeches back, the first time he uttered a thoughtful 'Mmmm.' That was when his attention began to wander, so that he was unable to give any concentration at all to two matters of enormous importance to him and Arlene: the impending trial and their marriage plans. What interested Carella more, however, was what Fletcher had said *after* he knew the place was wired. Certain of an audience now, knowing that whichever cop was actually monitoring the equipment, the tape or transcript would eventually get back to the investigating officer, Fletcher had:

(1) Suggested the possibility that Corwin was not guilty of the murder.
(2) Flatly stated that a cop named Carella suspected him of having killed his own wife.
(3) Expressed the admiration he felt for Carella while wondering if Carella was aware of it.
(4) Speculated that Carella, as a thorough cop, had already doped out the purpose of the bar-crawling last Sunday night, was cognizant of Sarah's promiscuity and knew that Fletcher was aware of it as well.
(5) Made a little joke about 'telling' Carella, when in fact he had already told him through the surveillance equipment in the apartment.

Carella felt as eerie as he had when lunching with Fletcher and later when drinking with him. Fletcher seemed to be playing a dangerous game, in which he taunted Carella with bits and pieces of knowledge, and dared him to fit them together into a meaningful whole that would prove he had slain Sarah. On the tape, Fletcher had said in an oddly gentle voice, 'I can understand his reasoning. I'm just not sure he can understand mine.' He had spoken these words after he knew the place was wired, and it could be assumed he was speaking them directly to Carella. But what was he trying to say? And why?

Carella wanted very much to hear what Fletcher would say when he *didn't* know he was being overheard. He asked Lieutenant Byrnes for permission to request a court order putting a bug in Fletcher's automobile. Byrnes granted permission, and the court issued the order. Carella called the Police Laboratory again, and was told that a technician would be assigned to him as soon as he found out where Fletcher parked his automobile.

Reading another man's love letters is like eating Chinese food alone.

In the comparative stillness of the squadroom, Kling joylessly picked over each of Richmond's separate tasty dishes, unable to share them, unable to comment on their flavor or texture. That they were interesting at *all* was a tribute to Richmond's cleverness; his letters were being censored before they left the prison, to make sure they did not contain requests for a file inside a birthday cake, and censorship can somewhat inhibit a man's ardor. As a result, Richmond could write only indirectly about his intense need for Nora, and his longing to rejoin her once he had served his sentence, which he fully expected to be reduced once he went before the parole board.

One letter, however, contained a short paragraph that read somewhat like an open threat:

I hope you are being true to me. Pete tells me he is sure this is so. He is there if you need him for anything, so don't hesitate to call. In any case, he will be watching over you.

Kling read the sentence yet another time, and was reaching for the telephone when it rang. He lifted the receiver.

'Eighty-seventh Squad, Kling.'

'Bert, this is Cindy.'

'Hi,' he said.

'Are you busy?' she asked.

'I was just about to call the IS.'

'Oh.'

'But go ahead. It can wait.'

Cindy hesitated. Then, her voice very low, she said, 'Bert, can I see you tomorrow?'

'Tomorrow?' he said.

'Yes.' She hesitated again. 'Tomorrow's Christmas Eve.'

'I know.'

'I bought something for you.'

'Why'd you do that, Cindy?'

'Habit,' she said, and he suspected she was smiling.

'I'd love to see you, Cindy,' he said.

'I'll be working till five.'

'No Christmas party?'

'At a *hospital*? Bert, my dear, we deal here daily with life and death.'

'Don't we all,' Kling said, and smiled. 'Shall I meet you at the hospital?'

'All right. The side entrance. That's near the emergency . . .'

'Yes, I know where it is. At five o'clock?'

'Well, five-fifteen.'

'Okay, five-fifteen.'

'You'll like what I got you,' she said, and then hung up. He was still smiling when he put his call through to the

Identification Section. A man named Reilly listened to his request, and promised to call back with the information in ten minutes. He called back in eight.

'Kling?' he said.

'Yes?'

'Reilly at the IS. I've got that packet on Frank Richmond. You want me to duplicate it or what?'

'Can you just read me his yellow sheet?'

'Well,' Reilly said, 'it's a pretty long one. The guy's been in trouble with the law since he was sixteen.'

'What kind of trouble?'

'Minor crap mostly. Except for the latest one.'

'When?'

'Two months ago.'

'What was the charge?'

'Armed robbery.'

Kling whistled, and then said, 'Have you got the details there, Reilly?'

'Not on his B-sheet. Let me see if there's a copy of the arrest report.'

Kling waited. On the other end, be could hear papers being shuffled. At last, Reilly said, 'Yeah, here it is. Him and another guy went into a supermarket along about closing time, ripped off the day's receipts. Got caught on the way out by an off-duty detective who lived in the neighborhood.'

'Who was the other guy?'

'Man named Jack Yancy. He's doing time too. You want me to pull his folder?'

'No, that's not necessary.'

'Third guy got off scot-free.'

'I thought you said there were only two of them.'

'No, there was an alleged wheel-man on the job, waiting in the parking lot near the delivery entrance. Caught him in the car with the engine running, but he claimed he didn't know anything about what was going on inside. Richmond and Yancy backed him, said they'd never seen him before in their lives.'

'Honor among thieves?' Kling said. 'I don't believe it.'

'Stranger things happen,' Reilly said.

'What's his name?'

'The wheel-man? Peter Brice.'

'Got an address for him?'

'Not on the report. You want me to hit the file again?'

'Would you?'

'I'll get back,' Reilly said, and hung up.

When the phone rang ten minutes later, Kling thought it would be Reilly again. Instead, it was Arthur Brown.

'Bert,' he said, 'the Orton woman just called Fletcher. Can you get in touch with Steve?'

'I'll try. What's up?'

'They made a date for tomorrow night. They're going across the river to a place named The Chandeliers. Fletcher's picking her up at seven-thirty.'

'Right,' Kling said.

'Bert?'

'Yeah?'

'Does Steve want me on this phone tap while they're out eating? Tomorrow's Christmas Eve, you know.'

'I'll ask him.'

'Also, Hal wants to know if he's supposed to sit in the truck all the while they're out.'

'Steve'll be in touch.'

'Because after all, Bert, if they're over in the next state eating, what's there to listen to in the apartment?'

'Right, I'm sure Steve'll agree.'

'Okay. How's everything up there?'

'Quiet.'

'Really?' Brown asked, and hung up.

15

The detective who engaged the garage attendant in a bullshit conversation about a hit-and-run accident was Steve Carella. The lab technician who posed as a mechanic sent by the Automobile Club to charge a faulty battery was the same man who had wired Arlene Orton's apartment.

Fletcher's car was parked in a garage four blocks from his office, a fact determined simply by following him to work that morning of December 24. (Carella had already figured that Fletcher would park the car where he finally *did* park it because the pattern had been established in the earlier surveillance; a man who drove to work each day generally parked his car in the same garage or lot.)

On the sidewalk outside the garage, Carella asked invented questions about a damaged left fender and headlight on a fictitious 1968 Dodge, while upstairs the lab technician was installing his bug in Fletcher's 1972 Oldsmobile. It would have been simpler and faster to put in a battery-powered FM transmitter similar to those he had installed in Arlene Orton's apartment, but since batteries needed constant changing, and since access to any given automobile was infinitely more difficult than access to an apartment, he decided on wiring his bug into the car's electrical system instead. With the hood open, with charge cables going to Fletcher's battery from his own tow-truck battery, he busily spliced and taped, tucked and tacked. He did not want to put the bug under the dashboard (the easiest spot) because this was wintertime, and the car heater would undoubtedly be in use, and the sensitive microphone would pick up every rattle and rumble of the heater instead of the conversation in the car. So he wedged the microphone into the front cushion, between seat and back, and then ran his wires under the car rug, and up under the dashboard, and finally into the electrical system. Within the city limits, the microphone would effectively broadcast any sound in the car for a distance of little more than a block, which meant that Fletcher's Oldsmobile would have to be closely followed by the monitoring unmarked police sedan. If Fletcher left the city, as he planned to do tonight when he took Arlene to The Chandeliers, the effective range of the transmitter on the open road would be about a quarter of a mile. In either case, the listener-pursuer had his work cut out for him.

On the sidewalk, Carella saw the technician drive out in his battered tow truck, abruptly thanked the garage attendant for his time, and headed back to the squadroom.

The holiday was starting in earnest and so, in keeping with the conventions of that festive season, the boys of the 87th Squad held their annual Christmas party at 4 P.M. that afternoon. The starting time for the party was entirely arbitrary, since it depended on when the squad's guests began dropping in. The guests, unlike those to be found at most other Christmas parties in the city, were in the crime business, mainly because the hosts were in that same business. Most of the guests were shoplifters. Some of them were pickpockets. A few of them were drunks. One of them was a murderer.

The shoplifters had been arrested in department stores

scattered throughout the precinct, the Christmas shopping season being a good time to lift merchandise, Christmas Eve being the last possible day to practice the art in stores still jammed to the rafters. The shoplifters plied their trade in various ways. A skinny lady shoplifter named Hester Brady, for example, came into the squadroom looking like a pregnant lady. Her pregnancy had been caused by stuffing some two hundred dollars' worth of merchandise into the overlarge bloomers she wore under her dress, a risky procedure unless one is skilled at lift, grab, stuff, drop the skirt, move to the next aisle, advance in the space of twenty minutes from a sweet Irish virgin to a lady eight months along; such are the vagaries of birth control.

A man named Felix Hopkins dressed for his annual shopping spree in a trenchcoat lined with dozens of pockets to accommodate the small and quite expensive pieces of jewelry he lifted from counters here and there. A tall, thin distinguished-looking black man with a tidy mustache and gold-rimmed spectacles, he would generally approach the counter and ask to see a cigarette lighter, indicating the one he wanted, and then rip off five or six fountain pens while the clerk was busy getting the lighter out of the display case. His hands worked as swiftly as a magician's; he had been at the job such a long time now that he didn't even have to unbutton the coat anymore. And though the pockets inside the coat now contained a gold fountain pen, a platinum watch, a gold money clip, a rhinestone necklace, an assortment of matched gold earrings, a leather-bound traveling clock, and a monogrammed ring with a black onyx stone, he still protested to the arresting officer that he had bought all these items elsewhere, had thrown away the sales slips, and was taking them home to wrap them himself because he didn't like the shitty job the stores did.

Most of the other shoplifters were junkies, desperate in

their need, unmindful of store detectives and city detectives, sorely tempted by the glittering display of goods in what was surely the world's largest marketplace, knowing only that whatever chances they took might net them a bag or two of heroin before nightfall, guarantee them a Christmas Day free from the pangs of drug-hunger and the pains of withdrawal. They were the pitiful ones, pacing the detention cage at the rear of the squadroom, ready to scream or vomit, knowing that being busted meant cold turkey for Christmas Day, with the only hope being methadone instead – maybe. They were looked upon with disdain by the haughty professionals like Hester Brady of the pregnant bloomers, Felix Hopkins of the pocketed raincoat, and Junius Cooper of the paper-stuffed packages.

Junius Cooper had figured out his dodge all by himself. He was a man of about forty-three, well-dressed, looking somewhat like a harried advertising executive who was rushing around picking up last-minute gifts his secretary had neglected to buy. He came into each department store carrying several shopping bags brimming with gift wrapped parcels. His *modus operandi* worked in two ways, both equally effective. In either instance, he would stand next to a man or woman who was legitimately shopping and who had momentarily put his own shopping bag on the floor or on the counter top. Junius would immediately: (a) transfer one of the legitimate shopper's gift-wrapped packages into his own shopping bag or (b) pick up the legitimate shopper's bag and leave his own bag behind in its place. The beautifully wrapped boxes in Junius' bag contained nothing but last Sunday's newspapers. His system was a bit potluckish, but it provided the advantage of being able to walk innocently past department-store cops, carrying packages actually paid for by bona-fide customers and wrapped by department-store clerks. It was almost impossible to catch Junius unless you saw him making the actual exchange. That was how he had been caught today.

This mixed bag of shoplifters mingled in the squadroom with their first cousins, the pickpockets, who similarly looked upon the frantic shopping days before Christmas as their busiest time of the year. A pickpocket enjoys nothing better than a crowd, and the approaching holiday brought the crowds out like cockroaches from under the bathroom sink: crowds in stores, crowds in the streets, crowds in the buses and subways. They worked in pairs or alone, these light-fingered artists, a nudge or a bump, an 'Oh, excuse me,' and a purse delicately lifted from a handbag, a hip pocket slit with a razor blade to release the bulging wallet within. There was not a detective in the city who did not carry his wallet in the left-hand pocket of his trousers, close to his balls, rather than in the sucker hip pocket; cops are not immune to pickpockets. They were surrounded by them that afternoon, all of them innocent, naturally, all of them protesting that they knew their rights.

The drunks did not know their rights, and did not particularly care about them. They had all begun celebrating a bit early and had in their exuberance done one thing or another considered illegal in this fair city – things like throwing a bus driver out onto the sidewalk when he refused to make change for a ten-dollar bill, or smashing the window of a taxicab when the driver said he couldn't possibly make a call to Calm's Point on the busiest day of the year, or kicking a Salvation Army lady who refused to allow her trombone to be played by a stranger, or pouring a quart of scotch into a mailbox, or urinating on the front steps of the city's biggest cathedral. Things like that. Minor things like that.

One of the drunks had killed someone.

He was unquestionably the star of the 87th's little Christmas celebration, a small man with vivid blue eyes and the hands of a violinist, beetling black brows, a mane of black hair, stinking of alcohol and vomit, demanding over and again to know just what the hell he was doing in a police station, even though there was blood all over his white shirt front and speckled on his pale face and staining his long thin, delicate fingers.

The person he had killed was his sixteen-year-old daughter.

He seemed to have no knowledge that she was dead. He seemed not to remember at all that he had come into his apartment at three o'clock that afternoon, little more than an hour ago, having begun his Christmas celebrating at the office shortly after lunch, and had found his daughter making love with a boy on the living-room sofa, the television casting unseen pictures into the darkened room, television voices whispering, whispering, and his daughter locked in embrace with a strange boy, skirts up over belly and thighs, buttocks pumping, ecstatic moans mingling with the whisper of television shadows, not hearing her father when he came into the room, not hearing him when he went into the kitchen and searched in the table drawer for a weapon formidable enough, punishing enough, found only a paring knife and discarded that as unequal to the task, discovered a hammer in the shoebox under the sink, hefted it on the palm of his hand, and, thin-lipped, went into the living room where his daughter still moaned beneath the weight of her young lover, and seized the boy by the shoulder and pulled him off her, and then struck her repeatedly with the hammer until the girl's face and head were gristle and pulp and the boy screamed until he fainted from exhaustion and shock and the woman next door ran in and found her neighbor still wielding the hammer in terrible dark vengeance for the unpardonable sin his daughter had committed on the day before Christmas. 'George,' she had whispered, and he had turned to her with blank eyes, and she had said, 'Oh, George, what have you done?' and he had dropped the hammer, and could not remember from that moment on what he had done.

It was a nice little Christmas party the boys of the 87th had.

He had forgotten, almost, what she looked like.

She came through the hospital's chrome and glass revolving doors, and he saw at first only a tall blond girl, full-breasted and wide-hipped, honey blond hair clipped close to her head, cornflower-blue eyes, shoving through the doors and out onto the low, flat stoop, and he reacted to her the way he might react to any beautiful stranger stepping into the crisp December twilight, and then he realized it was Cindy, and his heart lurched.

'Hi,' he said.

'Hi.'

She took his arm. They walked in silence for several moments.

'You look beautiful,' he said.

'Thank you. So do you.'

He was, in fact, quite aware of the way they looked together, and fell immediately into the Young Lovers syndrome, positive that everyone they passed on the windswept street knew instantly that they were mad about each other. Each stranger (or so he thought) cased them quickly, remarking silently on their oneness, envying their youth and strength and glowing health, longing to be these two on Christmas Eve, Cindy and Bert, American Lovers, who had met cute, and loved long, and fought hard, and parted sadly, and were now together again in the great tradition of the season, radiating love like flashing Christmas bulbs on a sixty-foot-high tree.

They found a cocktail lounge near the hospital, one they had never been to before, either together or separately, Kling sensing that a 'first' was necessary to their rediscovery of each other. They sat at a small round table in a corner of the room. The crowd noises were comforting. He suspected an English pub might be like this on Christmas Eve, the voice cadences lulling and soft, the room itself warm and protective, a good place for nurturing a love that had almost died and was now about to redeclare itself.

'Where's my present?' he said, and grinned in mock, evil greediness.

She reached behind her to where she had hung her coat on a wall peg, and dug into the pocket, and placed a small package in the exact center of the table. The package was wrapped in bright blue paper and tied with a green ribbon and bow. He felt a little embarrassed; he always did when receiving a gift. He went into the pocket of his own coat, and placed his gift on the table beside hers, a slightly larger package wrapped in jingle-bells paper, red and gold, no bow.

'So,' she said.

'So,' he said.

'Merry Christmas.'

'Merry Christmas.'

They hesitated. They looked at each other. They both smiled.

'You first,' he said.

'All right.'

She slipped her fingernail under the Scotch Tape and broke open the wrapping without tearing the paper, and then eased the box out, and moved the wrapping aside, intact, and centered the box before her, and opened its lid. He had bought her a plump gold heart, seemingly bursting with an inner life of its own, the antiqued gold chain a tether that kept it from ballooning ecstatically into space. She looked at the heart, and then glanced quickly into his expectant face and nodded briefly and said, 'Thank you, it's beautiful.'

'It's not Valentine's Day . . .'

'Yes.' She was still nodding. She was looking down at the heart again, and nodding.

'But I thought . . .' He shrugged.

'Yes, it's beautiful,' she said again. 'Thank you, Bert.'

'Well,' he said, and shrugged again, feeling vaguely uncomfortable and suspecting it was because he hated the ritual of opening presents. He ripped off the bow on her gift, tore open the paper, and lifted the lid off the tiny box. She had bought him a gold tie-tack in the form of miniature handcuffs, and he read meaning into the gift immediately, significance beyond the fact that he was a cop whose tools of the trade included real handcuffs hanging from his belt. His gift had told her something about the way he felt, and he was certain that her gift was telling him the very same thing – they were together again, she was binding herself to him again.

'Thank you,' he said.

'Do you like it, Bert?'

'I love it.'

'I thought . . .'

'Yes, I love it.'

'Good.'

They had not yet ordered drinks. Kling signaled for the waiter, and they sat in curious silence until he came to the table. The waiter left, and the silence lengthened, and it was then that Kling began to suspect something was wrong, something was terribly wrong. She had closed the lid on his gift, and was staring at the closed box.

'What is it?' Kling asked.

'Bert . . .'

'Tell me, Cindy.'

'I didn't come here to . . .'

He knew already, there was no need for her to elaborate.

He knew, and the noises of the room were suddenly too loud, the room itself too hot.

'Bert, I'm going to marry him,' she said.

'I see.'

'I'm sorry.'

'No, no,' he said. 'No, Cindy, please.'

'Bert, what you and I had together was very good . . .'

'I know that, honey.'

'And I just couldn't end it the way . . . the way we were ending it. I had to see you again, and tell you how much you'd meant to me. I had to be sure you knew that.'

'Okay,' he said.

'Bert?'

'Yes, Cindy. Okay,' he said. He smiled and touched her hand reassuringly. 'Okay,' he said again.

They spent a half hour together, drinking only the single round, and then they went out into the cold, and they shook hands briefly, and Cindy said, 'Good-bye, Bert,' and he said, 'Good-bye, Cindy,' and they walked off in opposite directions.

Peter Brice lived on the third floor of a brownstone on the city's South Side. Kling reached the building at a little past six-thirty, went upstairs, listened outside the door for several moments, drew his service revolver, and knocked. There was no answer. He knocked again, waited, holstered his revolver, and was starting down the hall when a door at the opposite end opened. A blond-headed kid of about eight looked into the hallway and said, 'Oh.'

'Hello,' Kling said, and started down the steps.

'I thought it might be Santa Claus,' the kid said.

'Little early,' Kling said over his shoulder.

'What time does he come?' the kid asked.

'After midnight.'

171

'When's that?' the kid shouted after him.

'Later,' Kling shouted back, and went down to the ground floor. He found the super's door alongside the stairwell, near where the garbage cans were stacked for the night. He knocked on the door and waited. A black man wearing a red flannel robe opened the door and peered into the dim hallway.

'Who is it?' he said, squinting up into Kling's face.

'Police officer,' Kling said. 'I'm looking for a man named Peter Brice. Know where I can find him?'

'Third-floor front,' the super said. 'Don't do no shootin' in the building.'

'He's not home,' Kling said. 'Got any idea where he might be?'

'He hangs out on the corner sometimes.'

'What corner?'

'Barbecue joint on the corner. Brice's brother works there.'

'Up the street here?'

'Yeah,' the super said. 'What'd he do?'

'Routine investigation,' Kling answered. 'Thanks a lot.'

The streets were dark. Last-minute shoppers, afternoon party-goers, clerks and shopgirls, workingmen and house-wives, all of whom had been rushing toward tomorrow since the day after Thanksgiving, now moved homeward to embrace it, put the final fillip on the tree, drink a bit of nog, spend the last quiet hours in peaceful contemplation before the onslaught of relatives and friends in the morning, the attendant frenzied business of gifting and getting. A sense of serenity was in the air. This is what Christmas is all about, Kling thought, this peaceful time of quiet footfalls, and suddenly wondered why the day before Christmas had some-how become more meaningful to him than Christmas Day itself.

Skewered, browning chickens turned slowly on spits, their

savory aroma filling the shop as Kling opened the door and stepped inside. A burly man in a white chef's apron and hat was behind the counter preparing to skewer four more plump white birds. He glanced up as Kling came in. Another man was at the cigarette machine, his back to the door. He was even bigger than the one behind the counter, with wide shoulders and a thick bull's neck. He turned from the machine as Kling closed the door, and the recognition between them was simultaneous. Kling knew at once that this was the man who'd beaten him senseless last Monday night, and the man knew that Kling had been his victim. A grin cracked across his face. 'Well, well,' he said, 'look who's here, Al.'

'Are you Peter Brice?' Kling asked.

'Why, yes, so I am,' Brice said, and took a step toward Kling, his fists already clenched.

Kling had no intention of getting into a brawl with a man as big as Brice. His shoulder still ached (Meyer's copper bracelet wasn't worth a damn) and he had a broken rib and a broken heart besides (which can also hurt). The third button of his overcoat was still unbuttoned. He reached into the coat with his right hand, seized the butt of his revolver, drew it swiftly and effortlessly, and pointed it directly at Brice's gut.

'Police officer,' he said. 'I want to ask you some questions about . . .'

The greasy skewer struck his gun hand like a sword, whipping down fiercely across the knuckles. He whirled toward the counter as the skewer came down again, striking him hard across the wrist, knocking the gun to the floor. In that instant Brice threw the full weight of his shoulder and arm into a punch that caught Kling close to his Adam's apple. Three things flashed through his mind in the next three seconds. First, he realized that if Brice's punch had landed an inch to the right, he would now be dead. Which meant that

Brice had no compunctions about sending him home in a basket. Next he realized, too late, that Brice had asked the man behind the counter to 'look who's here, Al.' And then he realized, also too late, that the super had said, 'Brice's brother works there.' His right wrist aching, the three brilliant flashes sputtering out by the time the fourth desperate second ticked by, he backed toward the door and prepared to defend himself with his one good hand, that one being the left and not too terribly good at all. Five seconds gone since Al had hit him on the hand (probably breaking something, the son of a bitch) and Pete had hit him in the throat. Al was now lifting the counter top and coming out front to assist his brother, the idea probably having occurred to both of them that, whereas it was not bad sport to kick around a jerk who was chasing after Frank Richmond's girl, it was bad news to discover that the jerk was a cop, and worse news to let him out of here alive.

The chances of getting out of here alive seemed exceedingly slim to Detective Bert Kling. Seven seconds gone now, ticking by with amazing swiftness as they closed in on him. This was a neighborhood where people got stomped into the sidewalk every day of the week and nary a soul ever paused to tip his hat or mutter a 'how-de-do' to the bleeding victim. Pete and Al could with immunity take Kling apart in the *next* seven seconds, put him on one of their chicken skewers, hang him on the spit, turn him and baste him in his own juices, and sell him later for sixty-nine cents a pound. Unless he could think of something clever.

He could not seem to think of a single clever thing.

Except maybe you shouldn't leave your undefended gun hand within striking distance of a brother with a greased skewer.

His gun was on the floor in the corner now, too far to reach.

(Eight seconds.)

The skewers were behind the counter, impossible to grab.

(Nine seconds.)

Pete was directly ahead of him, maneuvering for a punch that would knock Kling's head into the gutter outside. Al was closing in on the right, fists bunched.

(With a mighty leap, Detective Bert Kling sprang out of the pit.)

He wished he *could* spring out of the goddamn pit. He braced himself, feinted toward Pete, and then whirled suddenly to the right, where Al was moving in fast, and hit him with his left, hard and low, inches below the belt. Pete swung, and Kling dodged the blow, and then swiftly stepped behind the doubled-over Al, bringing his bunched fist down across the back of his neck in a rabbit punch that sent him sprawling flat across his own sawdust-covered floor.

One down, he thought, and turned just as Pete unleashed a haymaker that caught him on the side opposite the broken rib, thank God for small favors. He lurched back against the counter in pain, brought up his knee in an attempt to groin Pete, who was hip to the ways of the street and sidestepped gingerly while managing at the same time to clobber Kling on the cheek, bringing his fist straight down from above his head, as though he were holding a mallet in it.

I am going to get killed, Kling thought.

'Your brother's dead,' he said.

He said the words suddenly and spontaneously, the first good idea he'd had all week. They stopped Pete cold in his tracks, with his fist pulled back for the blow that could have ended it all in the next thirty seconds, smashing either the bridge of Kling's nose or his windpipe. Pete turned swiftly to look at his brother where he lay motionless in the sawdust. Kling knew a good thing when he saw one. He didn't try to hit Pete again, he didn't even try to kick him; he knew that any further attempts at trying to overpower him physically were doomed to end only one way, and he did not desire a little tag on his big toe. He dove headlong for his gun in the corner of the room, scooped it up in his left hand, the butt awkward and uncomfortable, rolled over, sat up, and curled his finger around the trigger as Pete turned toward him once again.

'Hold it, you son of a bitch!' Kling said.

Pete lunged across the room.

Kling squeezed the trigger once, and then again, aiming for Pete's trunk, just as he had done on the police range so many times, the big target up there at the end of the range, the parts of the body marked with numerals for maximum lethal reward, five points for the head and throat, chest and abdomen, four for the shoulders, three for the arms, two for the legs. He scored a ten with Peter Brice, because both slugs caught him in the chest, one of them going directly through his heart and the other piercing his left lung.

Kling lowered his gun.

He sat on the floor in the corner of the room, and watched Pete's blood oozing into the sawdust, and wiped sweat from his lip, and blinked, and then began crying because this was one hell of a fucking Christmas Eve, all right.

Carella had been parked across the street from The Chandeliers for close to two hours, waiting for Fletcher and Arlene to finish their dinner. It was now ten minutes to ten, and he was drowsy and discouraged and beginning to think the bug in the car wasn't such a hot idea after all. On the way out to the restaurant, Fletcher and Arlene had not once mentioned Sarah or the plans for their impending marriage. The only remotely intimate thing they had discussed was receipt of the lingerie Fletcher had sent, which Arlene just *adored*, and which she planned to model for him later that night.

It was now later that night, and Carella was anxious to put

them both to bed and get home to his family. When they finally came out of the restaurant and began walking toward Fletcher's Oldsmobile, Carella actually uttered an audible 'At *last*' and started his car. Fletcher started the Olds in silence, and then apparently waited in silence for the engine to warm before pulling out of the parking lot. Carella followed close behind, listening intently. Neither Fletcher nor Arlene had spoken a word since they entered the automobile. They proceeded east on Route 701 now, heading for the bridge, and still they said nothing. Carella thought at first that something was wrong with the equipment, and then he thought that Fletcher had tipped to *this* bug, too, and was deliberately maintaining silence, and then finally Arlene spoke and Carella knew just what had happened. The pair had argued in the restuarant, and Arlene had been smoldering until this moment when she could no longer contain her anger. The words burst into the stillness of Carella's car as he followed close behind, Arlene shouting, Maybe you don't want to marry me at *all*!

That's ridiculous, Fletcher said.

Then why won't you set a date? Arlene said.

I have set a date, Fletcher said.

You haven't set a date. All you've done is say after the trial, after the trial. *When* after the trial?

I don't know yet.

When the hell *will* you know, Gerry?

Don't yell.

Maybe this whole damn thing has been a stall. Maybe you *never* planned to marry me.

You know that isn't true, Arlene.

How do I know there really *were* separation papers?

There were. I told you there were.

Then why wouldn't she sign them?

Because she loved me.

Bullshit.

She said she loved me.

If she loved you . . .

She did.

Then why did she do those horrible things?

I don't know.

Because she was a whore, that's why.

To make me pay, I think.

Is that why she showed you her little black book?

Yes, to make me pay.

No. Because she was a whore.

I guess. I guess that's what she became.

Putting a little TG in her book every time she told you about a new one.

Yes.

A new one she'd fucked.

Yes.

Told Gerry, and marked a little TG in her book.

Yes, to make me pay.

A whore. You should have gone after her with detectives. Gotten pictures, threatened her, forced her to sign those damn . . .

No, I couldn't have done that. It would have ruined me, Arl.

Your precious career.

Yes, my precious career.

They both fell silent again. They were approaching the bridge now. The silence persisted. Fletcher paid the toll, and then drove onto the River Highway, Carella following. They did not speak again until they were well into the city. Carella tried to stay close behind them, but on occasion the distance between the two cars lengthened and he lost some words in the conversation.

You know she had me in a bind, Fletcher said. You know that, Arlene.

I thought so. But now I'm not so sure anymore.

She wouldn't sign the papers, and I (   ) adultery because (   ) have come out.

All right.

I thought (   ) perfectly clear, Arl.

And I thought (   )

I did everything I possibly could.

Yes, Gerry, but now she's dead. So what's your excuse now?

I have reasons for wanting to wait.

What reasons?

I told you.

I don't recall your telling me . . .

I'm suspected of having *killed* her, goddamn it!

(Silence. Carella waited. Up ahead, Fletcher was making a left turn, off the highway. Carella stepped on the accelerator, not wanting to lose voice contact now.)

What difference does that make? Arlene asked.

None at all, I'm sure, Fletcher said. I'm sure you wouldn't at all mind being married to a convicted murderer.

What are you talking about?

I'm talking about the possibility . . . never mind.

Let me hear it.

I said never mind.

I want to hear it.

All, right, Arlene. I'm talking about the possibility of someone accusing me of murder. And of having to stand trial for it.

That's the most paranoid . . .

It's not paranoid.

Then what is it? They've caught the murderer, they . . .

I'm only saying suppose. How could we get married if I killed her, if someone says I killed her?

No one has said it, Gerry.

Well, *if* someone should.

(Silence. Carella was dangerously close to Fletcher's car now, and risking discovery. But he could not afford to miss a word at this point, even if he had to follow bumper-to-bumper. On the floor of his own car, the unwinding reel of tape recorded each word of the dialogue between Fletcher and Arlene, admissible evidence if ever Fletcher were charged and brought to trial. Carella held his breath and stayed glued to the car ahead. When Arlene spoke again, her voice was very low.)

You sound as if you really *did* do it.

You know Corwin did it.

Yes, I know that. That's what . . . Gerry, I don't understand this.

There's nothing to understand.

Then why . . . if you *didn't* kill her, why are you so worried about being accused and standing trial and . . .

Someone could make a good case for it.

For what?

Someone could say I killed her.

Why would anyone do that? They know that Corwin . . .

They could say I came into the apartment and . . . they could say she was still alive when I came into the apartment.

Was she?

They could say it.

But who cares what they . . . ?

They could say the knife was still in her and I . . . I came in and found her that way and . . . finished her off.

Why would you do that?

To end it.

You wouldn't kill anyone, Gerry.

No.

Then why are you even suggesting such a terrible thing?

If she wanted it . . . if someone accused me . . . if someone said I'd done it . . . that I'd finished the job, pulled the knife across her belly . . . they could claim she *asked* me to do it.

What are you saying, Gerry?

Don't you see?

No. I don't.

I'm trying to explain that Sarah might have . . .

Gerry, I don't think I want to know.

I'm trying to tell you . . .

No, I don't want to know. Please, Gerry, you're frightening me, I really don't want to . . .

Listen to me, goddamn it! I'm trying to explain what *might* have happened, is that so fucking hard to accept? That she might have *asked* me to kill her?

Gerry, please, I . . .

I *wanted* to call the hospital, I was ready to call the hospital, don't you think I could *see* she wasn't fatally stabbed?

Gerry, Gerry, please . . .

She begged me to kill her, Arlene, she begged me to end it for her, she . . . damn it, can't *either* of you understand that? I tried to show him, I took him to all the places, I thought he was a man who'd understand. For Christ's sake, is it that difficult?

Oh my God, my God, *did* you kill her?

What?

Did you kill Sarah?

No. Not Sarah. Only the woman she'd become, the slut I'd forced her to become. She was Sadie, you see. When I killed her. When she died.

Oh my God, Arlene said, and Carella nodded in weary acceptance. He felt neither elated nor triumphant. As he followed Fletcher's car into the curb before Arlene's building, he experienced only a familiar nagging sense of repetition and despair. Fletcher was coming out of his car now, walking around to the curb side, opening the door for Arlene, who took his hand and stepped onto the sidewalk, weeping. Carella intercepted them before they reached the front door of the building. Quietly, he charged Fletcher with the murder of his wife, and made the arrest without resistance.

Fletcher did not seem at all surprised.

And so it was finished, or at least Carella thought it was.

In the silence of his living room, the children already asleep, Teddy wearing a long white hostess gown that reflected the colored lights of the Christmas tree, he put his arm around her and relaxed for the first time that day. The telephone rang at a quarter past one. He went into the kitchen, catching the phone on the third ring, hoping the children had not been awakened.

'Hello?' he said.

'Steve?'

He recognized the lieutenant's voice at once. 'Yes, Pete,' he said.

'I just got a call from Calcutta,' Byrnes said.

'Mmm?'

'Ralph Corwin hanged himself in his cell, just after midnight. Must have done it while we were still taking Fletcher's confession in the squadroom.'

Carella was silent.

'Steve?'

'Yeah, Pete.'

'Nothing,' Byrnes said, and hung up.

Carella stood with the dead phone in his hand for several seconds, and then replaced it on the hook. He looked into the living room, where the lights of the tree glowed warmly, and he thought of a despairing junkie in a prison cell, who had taken his own life without ever having known he had not taken the life of another.

It was Christmas Day.

Sometimes, none of it made any goddamn sense at all.